ESCAPING
the Giant Wave

BOOKS BY PEG KEHRET

Cages

Danger at the Fair

Deadly Stranger

Horror at the Haunted House

Night of Fear

Nightmare Mountain

Sisters, Long Ago

The Richest Kids in Town

Terror at the Zoo

FRIGHTMARES™: Backstage Fright

FRIGHTMARES™: Bone Breath and the Vandals

FRIGHTMARES™: Cat Burglar on the Prowl

FRIGHTMARES™: Don't Go Near Mrs. Tallie

FRIGHTMARES™: Desert Danger

FRIGHTMARES™: The Ghost Followed Us Home

FRIGHTMARES™: Race to Disaster

FRIGHTMARES™: Screaming Eagles

The Blizzard Disaster

The Flood Disaster

The Volcano Disaster

The Secret Journey

My Brother Made Me Do It

The Hideout

Saving Lilly

Available from Simon & Schuster

ESCAPING
the Giant Wave

PEG KEHRET

ALADDIN PAPERBACKS

New York   London   Toronto   Sydney

First Aladdin Paperbacks edition September 2004

ALADDIN PAPERBACKS
An imprint of Simon & Schuster
Children's Publishing Division
1230 Avenue of the Americas
New York, NY 10020

Also available in a Simon & Schuster Books for Young Readers hardcover edition.
Designed by Daniel Roode
The text of this book was set in Bembo.

Printed in the United States of America.
10 9 8 7 6 5 4 3 2

The Library of Congress has cataloged the hardcover edition as follows:
Kehret, Peg.
Escaping the giant wave / by Peg Kehret.
p. cm.
Summary: When an earthquake creates a tsunami while thirteen-year-old Kyle is babysitting his sister during a family vacation at a Pacific Coast resort, he tries to save himself, his sister, and a boy who has bullied him for years.
ISBN 0-689-85272-X (hc.)
[1. Tsunamis—Fiction. 2. Earthquakes—Fiction. 3. Natural disasters—Fiction. 4. Brothers and sisters—Fiction. 5. Bullies—Fiction. 6. Pacific Coast (Or.)—Fiction.] I. Title.
PZ7.K2518 Es 2003
[Fic]—dc21 2002152822
ISBN 0-689-85273-8 (Aladdin pbk.)

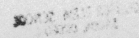

A *tsunami* (pronounced sue-NAH-mee) is a series of destructive ocean waves, usually started by earthquakes. Tsunamis can also be caused by underwater landslides or underwater volcanic eruptions.

1

"If you could change one thing about your life, what would it be?"

No one in my sixth-grade class answered our teacher. I could think of lots of things about my life that I'd like to change but I wasn't going to say them out loud, not even on the last day of school.

"Think about it. What do you wish was different?" Mrs. Hoke asked.

"I wish I was six feet tall," my friend Gary said.

Everyone, including Mrs. Hoke, laughed. Then she said, "I want you each to write down four goals for your summer. They must be goals that you can work to achieve, not something over which you have no control, such as getting taller. You don't have to turn your lists in. They are to help you improve yourselves."

I think Mrs. Hoke's goal was to keep the class out

of mischief without having a bunch of papers to correct.

I wrote my name, Kyle Davidson, at the top of a sheet of notebook paper and started my list:

1. Raise my batting average over .250
2. Learn to pop a wheelie on my scooter
3. Get Mom and Dad to increase my allowance

"Think before you write," Mrs. Hoke said. "Good goals have a long-term effect. A goal accomplished makes your life better."

I put one elbow on my desk, rested my chin on my palm, and read my list. Yes. My life would definitely be better if my batting average went up, if I could pop a wheelie, and if I had more money.

I was confident that I could achieve numbers one and two. All I needed was practice.

Number three would be more of a challenge. I planned to mention frequently to my parents how much spending money my friends have. I would remind them that I feed Alexander the Greatest, our cat, and clean his litter box every night. I also carry out the garbage and make popcorn for the whole family when we rent a movie. I figured if I kept talking about how helpful I am, I'd wear Mom and Dad down, and they'd agree to give me more allowance.

As I stared at my list, a hand shoved my elbow off the desk. My head jerked forward. "Ooof!" I said as I dropped my pencil.

Behind me, I heard Daren Hazelton snicker. I didn't need to turn around in order to know who had yanked my elbow.

I sighed, retrieved the pencil, and finished my list.

4. Make Daren Hazelton leave me alone

As soon as I wrote it, I put my hand over that line, in case Daren peeked at my paper.

Daren is the meanest kid in Edison School. He's probably the meanest kid in the world. I bet Daren was born mean. He probably bit the other babies and kicked the nurses before his parents took him home from the hospital.

I met Daren when I was five, on my first day of kindergarten. He came up behind me and bonked me on the head with a box of crayons. I didn't want to be labeled as either a crybaby or a tattletale on my first day of school, so I walked away from Daren without saying or doing anything, and I didn't tell the teacher on him.

Big mistake.

From then on, Daren sneaked up on me once every day. He punched me, poked me with a pencil, tripped me, and shoved me. He never hurt me enough that I had to go to the school nurse—he was too devious for that. His punches stung but didn't bruise me; his pokes left an indentation but never broke the skin.

By the time I got to first grade, being bullied by Daren had become a regular part of my day. It still is.

I never punched him back because Daren always outweighed me by plenty. Now that we're both finishing sixth grade, he stands five feet seven and is built like a brick wall, while I'm barely five feet tall and as skinny as a ruler.

Size was only part of the reason I ignored Daren all those years. I dislike confrontations of any kind, and I avoid physical conflict most of all. I don't even like to watch boxing or wrestling on TV.

Fighting just isn't my way of handling a problem and for the most part that's a good thing. When I'm dealing with reasonable people I can settle any differences with discussion and compromise.

Daren Hazelton is not a reasonable person.

Daren Hazelton is a mean, big, strong troublemaker.

I'm not the only one Daren hassles. He picks on the younger kids, and I've seen him start fights with older boys in the seventh and eighth grades. Some kids fight back and others complain to their teachers.

Daren probably holds the school record for getting sent to the principal's office the most times, but that hasn't slowed him down one bit.

I used to tell myself that brains are more important than brawn and that by avoiding a fight I was outsmarting Daren. Lately, though, I haven't felt smart; I've felt like a coward. It was time to stand up to Daren at last and put an end to his sneak attacks. The question was, how?

"Read your goals once a week during the summer," Mrs. Hoke said. "Good luck in achieving your ambitions."

It will take more than luck, I thought as I folded my list and stuck it in my notebook.

I wouldn't see Daren during vacation, so I had three months to figure out a workable plan to keep him from punching me again next year. I decided to concentrate on my other three goals first, and worry about Daren in August.

That afternoon I took home a year's accumulation of items from my locker, including a petrified apple core, a coupon good for twenty cents off a bag of jellybeans (expiration date: two months ago), three overdue library books, and a pair of dirty socks that I didn't put on after gym class one day when I was in a hurry. My backpack bulged. I would have tossed some of it away at school, but all the wastebaskets there were already overflowing with other kids' trash.

I was eating graham crackers and sorting through all the junk, when Mom made a surprise announcement.

"Due to your maturity and responsible behavior, Dad and I have decided that it is no longer necessary to hire a sitter for you and BeeBee."

BeeBee is my little sister and yes, that is her real name. Mom and Dad couldn't decide whether to name her Bernice, after Dad's mother, or Barbara, after Mom's mother, so they took the two initials and made up a brand-new weirdo name.

If the two Bs stood for Brainy and Bizarre, the name would fit her perfectly. BeeBee is not your ordinary eight-year-old. Not by a long shot.

When Mom gave me the no-more-baby-sitter news, she smiled expectantly, and I could tell she thought I would be glad.

"How much?" I asked.

Mom seemed baffled. "How much what?"

"How much do I get paid for watching BeeBee?"

"Paid!" Mom looked as if I had demanded a fee for making my bed or brushing my teeth.

"You always paid Shelly five dollars an hour," I said.

"That was different. Shelly was a hired sitter. You are . . ."

"A slave."

"Kyle, don't be ridiculous. You are a member of this family. We each contribute what we can, and you can help by taking care of BeeBee tomorrow night while your dad and I attend the monthly sales dinner."

My parents both work for a large real estate firm. Dad sells commercial office space; Mom sells houses and condominiums.

"How long will you be gone?" I asked.

"We need to leave at six," Mom said, "and we should be home by ten. Ten-thirty at the latest."

"From six until ten-thirty," I said. "That's four-and-a-half hours. Shelly would get paid twenty-two dollars and fifty cents."

"All you have to do is heat up dinner, wash the dishes, and see that BeeBee goes to bed at eight-thirty. It will be a snap."

"Shelly gets a tip for doing the dishes," I said.

"Shelly doesn't live here." Mom raised one eyebrow and gave me a look that suggested I wouldn't live here much longer either if I said another word about Shelly.

"What if BeeBee won't?" I asked.

"Won't what?"

"Won't eat her dinner. Won't go to bed. Won't do anything I say."

"I'll talk to her before we leave," Mom said. "I'll tell her that when she's all tucked in bed, you'll read to her for awhile."

My sister knows how to read but she still loves to have someone read aloud to her, especially if she gets to choose the reading material.

"I won't read one of her financial reports," I said. "I'll read part of a Harry Potter book or something else that normal kids like, but I am not reading about a mutual fund or the quarterly report from General Electric or any of BeeBee's other favorites."

My sister is a financial whiz. When she was two, she refused to play with blocks or dolls; all she wanted was a calculator.

Last Christmas when she went to get her picture taken with Santa, she asked him to bring her shares of stock in a toy company. "Toys break," BeeBee explained. "Stock appreciates."

"I'll try," the startled Santa said, "but I can't promise."

"You can choose what you read to her," Mom said. Then she added, "I'll make homemade pizza."

I knew the pizza was a thank you for me. Pizza is my all-time favorite food, especially Mom's homemade pizza, which she usually makes only for birthdays. Even so, I couldn't resist saying, "Let's see. Four-and-a-half hours times zero cents an hour equals . . ." I paused for dramatic effect. "Unfair."

BeeBee came in from the backyard, carrying her radio and her stuffed bear, Bill. The bear was named for Bill Gates, founder of Microsoft and BeeBee's hero because he's one of the richest people in the world. "The DOW is up thirty points," she said, smiling broadly, "and the NASDAQ is up ten. Bill and I are happy."

Nobody knows why BeeBee is interested in the stock market. It certainly isn't because our family is wealthy. We don't own any stocks, but BeeBee follows the daily stock market reports the way other kids read the cartoons. She is fascinated by the idea of many people owning a small share of a big company.

BeeBee put her radio and Bill on my bed, then helped herself to some graham crackers.

"Dad and I are going to a sales dinner tomorrow night," Mom said.

"Who's baby-sitting?" BeeBee asked.

"Kyle."

BeeBee choked and made a face as if the crackers were moldy. "No way," she sputtered. "Kyle isn't old enough."

"Kyle is thirteen," Mom said. "That's how old Shelly was when she began baby-sitting."

"How much?" BeeBee asked.

Mom gave her a suspicious look. "How much what?"

"How much do I get paid for letting Kyle be my sitter?"

"The sitter gets paid," I said, "not the sittee."

"Nobody is being paid," Mom said.

"Unfair," said BeeBee.

"That's what I told her," I said. "There ought to be special child labor laws for family members." Then I added, "Of course, if I were to get a bigger allowance, I might feel differently."

"I'll think about it," Mom said.

That wasn't *yes* but it wasn't *no*, either. Maybe I really would accomplish my summer goals.

As soon as Mom and Dad left the next evening, I told BeeBee, "I'm in charge now, and these are the rules."

She glared at me.

"Rule number one: We can eat dessert first."

BeeBee quit scowling.

"Rule number two: When we have pizza, we can eat it with our fingers instead of using a fork."

BeeBee smiled.

"Rule number three: The only required vegetables are baby carrots dipped in ranch dressing."

"This is going to be fun," BeeBee said.

It *was* fun, although I didn't tell Mom and Dad that. I wanted them to think they were taking advantage of me. I thought if they felt guilty, they would raise my allowance. Dream on.

I had been contributing my mature baby-sitting skills to the good of the family for about a month (with still no raise in my allowance) when Dad brought home a handful of travel brochures.

"We're going on a vacation," he said, "to the Oregon coast!"

"Did you win the lottery?" I asked.

"Lottery tickets are a waste of money," BeeBee said. "The odds of winning are terrible."

"I'm the Salesman of the Year," Dad said. "Mom and I get our expenses paid to a national sales conference in Fisher Beach, Oregon, and we're taking you along."

"How do we get there?" BeeBee asked.

"We're flying."

"All right!" I said. I'd never been on an airplane. In fact I had never been out of Kansas.

"Five days in the beautiful Pacific Northwest," Mom said. "Fresh crab and salmon. Rugged scenery. Look at the hotel where we'll be staying!" She unfolded one of the brochures.

BeeBee and I gazed at a picture of fir trees lining a curved driveway that led to a lodge built of logs. Each room overlooked the Pacific Ocean and had a stone fireplace. Baskets of pinecones and red apples adorned the bedside tables. Another picture, labeled "nature trail," showed a path curving uphill through native plants toward a forest of tall trees.

BeeBee squinted at the fine print. "Yikes!" she said. "Rooms start at three hundred seventy-five dollars a night!"

"The room is paid for as part of my prize," Dad said.

"That's what's so exciting," Mom said. "We would never stay in a place like this if we had to pay for it ourselves."

"Is there a Motel 6 in Fisher Beach?" BeeBee asked.

The only time our family ever stays in a motel is when we go to visit Mom's parents. They live in a one-bedroom apartment, so we always sleep at a nearby Motel 6.

"Frontier Lodge will be far more elegant than the Motel 6," Dad said.

"This is a first-class hotel," Mom added. "It's brand new and has two swimming pools, one indoor and one outdoor."

"If there is a Motel 6 in town," BeeBee said, "you could take the three hundred seventy-five dollars per night that the fancy lodge would cost, and instead of staying there, we'd stay at the Motel 6, and then with the money we save we could buy tax-free municipal bonds."

The rest of us stared at BeeBee.

"We could probably save three hundred dollars per night, times five nights." BeeBee paused while she did the math in her head. "That's fifteen hundred dollars!"

"I appreciate your frugality," Mom said, "but this is supposed to be a vacation where we feel pampered and special. We are going to enjoy the atmosphere of a deluxe hotel."

"Not that there's anything wrong with Motel 6," Dad said. "It's fine for when we visit Grandma and Grandpa."

"It's great when we're paying the bill," Mom said.

"Suit yourself," BeeBee said. "If it were my choice, I'd take the money and buy bonds."

"If it were your choice," I said, "we'd probably ask for cash and skip the trip altogether."

"No," BeeBee said. "I want to go to Oregon and see the ocean and hunt for shells. But the beach will be the same no matter where we sleep."

As it turned out, we should have taken BeeBee's suggestion. Of course, it's always easy to know the right choice after it's too late to go back and change your mind. Figuring out the right choice ahead of time is the hard part.

2

We spent the next three weeks planning our dream vacation. Mom wanted to walk on the beach, I wanted to tour a cheese factory, and Dad planned to visit an airplane museum.

BeeBee kept asking if we could rent a car and drive north into Washington state so she and Bill could see the Microsoft headquarters in Redmond, Washington. Luckily, Redmond was too far away.

"I hope you won't mind being our sitter one night, Kyle," Mom said. "For the 'Salespersons of the Year' celebration, the company has rented a huge private yacht, the *Elegant Empress*."

"The ship will leave in mid-afternoon on the second day we're there," Dad said. "We'll cruise until sunset, when a buffet dinner will be served followed by the award presentations."

"The cruise is the only part of the vacation that

doesn't include you kids," Mom said. "I'm sorry, but the invitation says 'adults only.'"

"That's okay," I said. "We don't want to listen to a bunch of speeches, anyway."

"You and BeeBee can get pizza from room service that night," Mom said, "and rent a video to watch in our room."

Mom and Dad still had not caught on that I liked being the one in charge, so I pretended that I was doing them a big favor when I agreed to baby-sit during our vacation. Maybe if they thought I was being especially cooperative, they would let me buy a really good souvenir.

"How much does it cost to rent the *Elegant Empress*?" BeeBee asked.

"I have no idea," Dad said.

"A lot," Mom said.

I picked up Bill the bear and made my voice high, pretending to be my sister. "You could rent a fleet of rowboats instead," I said, "and feed everyone a sandwich instead of the buffet dinner. Then you could use the money you save to buy presents for your children."

"Very funny," said Dad.

"Good idea," said BeeBee. "Except forget the

rowboats. Give everyone a life jacket and let them float in the water."

We all cracked up at the idea of Dad getting his award as he floated around in the ocean.

"This will be the best vacation ever," I said.

"The best vacation in the whole world," BeeBee agreed.

The Saturday of our departure for Oregon finally arrived, and even though we had to leave the house at five o'clock in the morning to get to the airport on time, I woke up before my alarm went off. Our family had never taken this kind of trip before. Usually we camp at a state park or visit relatives. I tried to look nonchalant at the airport, as if I flew somewhere every week, but I was so excited I couldn't sit still while we waited to board.

I was standing at the big windows, watching planes taxi down the runway, when someone punched me from behind.

"Hey, Kyle. I hear you're heading for Oregon too."

I recognized the voice, and the punch. Daren Hazelton.

"What are you doing here?" I asked as I rubbed my shoulder.

"Same as you," Daren said. "Going to Oregon with my mom and dad for the real estate convention."

No! I thought. *Say it isn't so.*

I said, "I didn't know your parents sold real estate."

"There are lots of things you don't know," Daren said.

"Where are you staying?" I asked.

"Some new hotel."

"The Frontier Lodge?" I crossed my fingers. *Please say no,* I thought. *Please, please stay anywhere except at my hotel.*

"Yeah, that's it," Daren said. "The Frontier Lodge."

My plans for a carefree vacation flew away faster than the jet outside the window. With Daren on the scene, I would spend my time trying to avoid getting punched, or tripped, or shoved into the pool, or worse.

One of Dad's Oregon brochures showed a picture of some loggers beside a huge cedar tree. An image of Daren with a chain saw buzzed across my mind.

I backed away from Daren toward my parents, knowing he would not hit me again in front of them.

Mom and Dad were talking with another couple. Mom waved me over to them, then introduced me to Mr. and Mrs. Hazelton, Daren's parents. "Mrs. Hazelton works for the online branch of our company," Dad said. "She's the Virtual Salesperson of the Year."

"Congratulations," I mumbled.

"I understand my son is a classmate of yours," Mrs. Hazelton said.

I nodded.

"Isn't that the best luck?" Mom said. "You'll have someone to pal around with on the beach."

I imagined Daren sneaking up behind me and shoving me into the water, or pushing me face first into the wet sand.

I forced a smile. "I'm not planning to spend much time at the beach," I said.

Mom looked surprised, since I had been talking for days about searching for shells or unusual driftwood that I could take home, to show my friends that I'd been to the Pacific Ocean.

Before Mom could say more, the airline announced that passengers in rows thirty to forty-five could begin boarding the plane. We quit talking and waited for our row to be called.

Daren and his parents sat three rows ahead of us.

I played cards with BeeBee during the flight, used the earphones to listen to music, and ate everything the steward brought.

"Free soft drinks," I said to BeeBee as the steward handed each of us a glass of crushed ice and a can of 7-Up. "This is great."

"They aren't free," BeeBee said.

"Sure they are," I said. "You only have to pay if you want wine or beer." I pointed at a man across the aisle who was handing the steward money in exchange for a glass of wine.

BeeBee said, "The cost of soft drinks is figured into the price of our ticket. We've already paid for them in advance."

"Oh," I said. I knew she was right, but it was more fun to think they were free.

After the plane landed in Portland, we took a special convention bus to Fisher Beach. Daren and his parents rode the bus too, but I took the seat farthest from the door and BeeBee sat next to me, so I was temporarily spared any more contact with Daren.

As we rode along, I gave myself a pep talk. This vacation was the perfect opportunity to make Daren quit bullying me. If I stood up to him the first time he bothered me on this trip, then I'd be able to enjoy the rest of my time in Oregon. But if I let him get away with anything, I'd spend the whole week wondering where he was and what he was up to. I didn't want to spend the first really good vacation of my life hiding from Daren, so I knew I had to take some action.

I remembered my summer goals. Here it was, the middle of July, and my batting average was stuck at .220, my scooter had a broken wheel, and my raise in allowance was still in the "we'll see" category. It was time to deal with Daren.

The bus dropped most of the passengers at hotels in the town of Fisher. When we finally arrived at the Frontier Lodge, my family, the Hazeltons, and one other couple were the only people left.

By then I had resolved to put an end to Daren's pranks. The next time he punched me, or pushed me, or did any of his revolting tricks, I was going to speak up. With both of our parents nearby, I should be able to talk back to Daren without getting maimed.

The Frontier Lodge didn't look much like the drawings in the brochure. Instead of a driveway lined with fir trees, there was a plywood sidewalk of the kind that's used around temporary construction sites. The word "LOBBY" and an arrow had been spray painted with red paint on the plywood.

A yellow bulldozer rumbled back and forth, scraping the area where the nature trail should have been. A flatbed truck held containers of shrubs to be planted.

I saw Mom look uneasily at Dad, who was frowning as he followed the red arrows toward the lobby.

"Welcome to the first-class hotel," I told BeeBee.

"We should ask for a refund," BeeBee said. "There isn't any water in the swimming pool." She pointed at a large concrete hole in the ground that was surrounded by a six-foot wire fence.

We walked beneath scaffolding and finally reached the lobby, where three workers with staple guns were noisily laying carpet. A too-cheerful person greeted us: "Welcome to Frontier Lodge!"

"We have reservations," Dad told the woman behind the desk, "but we didn't know the hotel was still under construction."

"We were delayed by a labor dispute," the woman said. "You'll be staying across the street at the Totem Pole Inn. I'm sure you'll be most comfortable there."

"Why weren't we notified?" Mom said. "We're supposed to attend a convention here."

"Our convention and dining facilities are ready and your meetings will be held as planned," the woman said, "but our guest suites didn't get finished. I'm sorry for the inconvenience. We were lucky to find rooms for all of the convention registrants who had planned to stay here. Many of them are at hotels in town; at least you are within walking distance of your meetings." She said it as if we should be grateful rather than disappointed.

"We ought to get a discount on the room," BeeBee said. "Being across the street from the convention is not as good as being in the same hotel. What if it rains?"

The woman behind the counter leaned forward and glared at BeeBee.

"There's no nature trail," BeeBee said, "and no water in the swimming pool. That's false advertising."

"She's right," Dad said. "The rate we were given was for a brand new hotel, with the convention meetings on site. We shouldn't have to pay the same rate for older, less convenient accommodations."

By now Daren and his parents, and the other couple from the bus, were in line behind us. The woman at the counter lowered her voice and said, "I can give you a special rate of two hundred fifty dollars per night."

"That will be fine," Dad said.

BeeBee grinned. I knew she was figuring out how much the discount had saved Dad's company. One hundred twenty-five dollars per night times five nights equals seven hundred twenty-five dollars!

I gave BeeBee a thumbs up.

A bellhop piled our bags on a luggage cart and pulled it down the plywood walkway. As we left the lobby, we heard Mrs. Hazelton yelling at the desk clerk, demanding to stay at the Frontier Lodge. Daren's voice joined his mother's. "I want to stay *here*," he whined. "You promised!"

I hoped the clerk would give in and find a room for the Hazeltons. That way Daren would be across the street from me rather than in the same hotel.

"This situation must be hard for you," Dad said to the bellhop.

"Most people are understanding," he said. "A few get obnoxious and insist they're going to stay in the new hotel whether the rooms are ready or not. When they find out the beds haven't been delivered yet, they change their minds."

We crossed the street to a much older hotel that was only three stories high.

"The Totem Pole Inn will be torn down as soon as the construction is finished on the lodge," the bellhop told us. "This land will be used for a parking garage, a restaurant, and some shops. There'll be an overhead walkway across the street to the hotel and conference center."

"How old is the Totem Pole Inn?" Mom asked.

"It was one of the first luxury hotels in Oregon," the man replied. "Built in 1928. Three American presidents have stayed here, and so have many movie stars. It's always been popular with celebrities because it's so far away from town. If you like quiet, this is the place to be, especially now when the inn is officially closed. The only guests are the few whose rooms weren't ready at the Frontier Lodge and who couldn't get rooms at one of the hotels in town."

"We weren't told when we registered that the hotel's being torn down," Dad said.

"You should have asked for a bigger discount," BeeBee said.

We entered the dimly lit lobby. I could tell it had once been an elegant facility, but it looked as if no upkeep had been done in several years. Wallpaper curled at the edges, and the frayed carpet had bare spots between the door and the elevator.

"It's not exactly what we were expecting," Mom said.

"We don't have to do anything here except sleep,"

Dad said, but I could tell he was disappointed too.

"We could have slept at a Motel 6," BeeBee said, "for a lot less money."

The bellhop pushed the "up" button on the elevator, and we all looked expectantly at the doors. They stayed closed. He pushed the button again, but it didn't light up.

"Looks like the elevator is out of order again," he said. "Do you mind walking up to the third floor, or do you want to wait in the lobby while I call the repair service?"

"Are there any first-floor rooms?" Dad asked.

"None that still have furniture."

"We'll walk up," Mom said.

The bellhop couldn't take the cart full of luggage up the stairs, so he carried Mom and Dad's bags while BeeBee and I each carried our own.

Two full flights of stairs later, we puffed into our room.

BeeBee ran to the window to look at the ocean view, Mom checked out the bathroom, Dad tipped the bellhop, and I stood in the doorway watching Daren and his parents walk toward me.

They stopped at a room three doors down the hall. My dream vacation was beginning to seem like a nightmare.

3

The next day we saw the warning sign.

We got up early, partly because we were too excited to sleep late and partly because our bodies were still on Kansas time, which was two hours later than Oregon. The construction noise from the new hotel hadn't helped either.

After breakfast at the Frontier Lodge, Mom, Dad, BeeBee, and I headed for the ocean. Wooden steps zigzagged from the hotel parking lot down to the beach.

"Twenty-seven steps," BeeBee said when we reached the bottom.

"It'll seem like more when we go up," Dad said.

The Pacific Ocean was awesome, stretching into the distance as far as I could see. A wide sandy beach, dotted with shells deposited at high tide, invited us to explore. Waves lapped the shore, sandpipers scuttled along just beyond the water's reach, and gulls swooped overhead.

The water was too cold for swimming, but BeeBee and I took off our shoes and socks, rolled up our pant legs, and waded along the edge.

BeeBee carried a plastic bucket; she began collecting shells and pretty stones.

"Be selective," Dad said. "You can't keep every rock you find."

"I don't plan to keep any of them," BeeBee said. "When we get home, I'm going to sell them to the other kids. Genuine Pacific Ocean souvenirs: ten cents each."

I saw Dad roll his eyes at Mom, and I was pretty sure they wouldn't let her sell the stones to her friends, but they didn't scold her now.

The tide was low, exposing wide outcrops of rock. Tide pools held tiny crabs, sea anemones, and even one starfish. I was tempted to put the sea creatures in BeeBee's bucket to take home, but I didn't do it. I wanted them to live more than I wanted to show them to my friends.

We walked and walked and saw only four other people. Each time a person approached, I looked to see if it was Daren and was relieved when it wasn't.

Mom said, "It's so beautiful here; I'm sorry to see a big hotel built. By next summer, this beach will probably be crowded."

"There's a sign sticking out of the sand," BeeBee said. She ran ahead to see what it said, then rushed back to report, "It's a warning sign! It says the Oregon coast might get hit by a t-s-u-n-a-m-i." She spelled out the word.

"Tsunami," I said. "It's a giant wave, usually caused by an earthquake."

BeeBee scowled at me. "How do you know that?" she asked. It always bugs her when I know something she doesn't.

"We did a disaster unit in fifth grade. Remember my report on volcanoes, when I made the model of Mount Saint Helens?"

BeeBee nodded.

"Gary gave his report on tsunamis. He enlarged some pictures that he had found in a book. They showed an area where a tsunami had hit. There were collapsed buildings and uprooted trees, but the photos were all taken a long time ago in Hawaii. I didn't know tsunamis ever happened in Oregon."

"Neither did I," said Mom. "The one I remember reading about was years ago in Alaska."

"Tsunamis sound scary," BeeBee said.

We gathered around the sign while Dad read it out loud. It said that tsunamis are dangerous, have

struck the Oregon coast many times, and can follow within minutes of an earthquake.

"Minutes!" Mom said. "That doesn't give much
time to get away."

Dad continued to read. "Most tsunamis are not
one giant wave, but a series of large waves that
strike the shore over the course of several hours."

"It had better not happen while we're here,"
BeeBee said. "I'd hate to think Dad's boss paid all
that money for our vacation and then we can't stay
because of a tsunami."

"We aren't any more likely to have a tsunami
while we're here than to be caught in a tornado
back home," Mom said.

"I wonder if they have tsunami drills in school
here," BeeBee said, "the way we have tornado drills."

"Probably," Dad said.

The sign had a map showing that the offshore
earthquake-prone area ran parallel to the coast of
Oregon.

"Where's Fisher Beach?" I asked.

Dad pointed to the center of the map. "Here's the
town of Fisher, and here's Fisher Beach."

"Great," I said. "We're right in the middle of the
danger zone."

Dad read the instructions for escaping a tsunami:

"Protect yourself during the earthquake. As soon as it stops, go inland and uphill. Do not go to the beach, even after a tsunami wave hits. Wait for official notice that it's safe before returning to the beach." He quit reading and looked at us. "You got that?"

We all nodded.

"Okay. Let's forget about giant waves and enjoy ourselves."

We walked awhile longer, then turned back toward the hotel. When we reached the zigzag steps again, Mom and Dad sat on some driftwood and watched the waves while BeeBee searched for shells.

I decided to make a "sea picture." I gathered stones, bits of seaweed, pieces of driftwood, two bird feathers, and some broken shells. I drew a rectangular "picture frame" in the sand with a stick and then used all the other materials to create my artwork. It turned out so well that I was sorry I had made it close to the water, where the tide would come in and wash it away. I decided to take a photo of the sea picture.

I went back to our room, got my camera, and was waiting for the elevator when Daren came out of his room. "What're you doing?" he asked.

"I'm meeting my folks down on the beach."

"I'll come with you."

I couldn't very well tell him no. It's a public beach. Still, my palms got sweaty at the idea of going anywhere with Daren.

When the elevator came, Daren got on first. Being shut in an elevator alone with him did not appeal to me, so I blurted, "I'll meet you downstairs. I need the exercise."

The elevator doors closed. I clumped down the stairs, reminding myself that this was my chance to fulfill one of my summer goals. Stand up to Daren. Put him in his place, once and for all.

Dream on.

I wanted to do it—but not now.

When I reached the lobby I looked at the elevator, expecting Daren to step out. The doors remained closed. Had he already gotten out and was hiding somewhere, waiting to pounce on me? I glanced nervously behind a large potted plant.

Then I noticed the arrow over the elevator that showed which floor it was on. The arrow was between two and three, and not moving. I pushed the "down" button but it didn't light up. The elevator was stuck.

I ought to leave him there, I thought. Payback for

seven years of punching me. I could pretend I thought he was ahead of me and go on down to the beach, and then when I saw him again, I'd ask why he hadn't come with me and act surprised when he said the elevator had stopped.

Then I thought how scary it would be to get stuck in an elevator, and I couldn't do it, not even to Daren.

I went to the counter in the lobby and rang the brass bell. When the clerk arrived I said, "There's a kid stuck in the elevator."

"Not again." The clerk sighed, as if the personal inconvenience was more than he could bear. "I suppose I should call the repair service." He sighed again.

"That seems like a good idea," I said. Then, having done what I could for Daren, I headed for the beach. I stopped several times to pick up more stones and another feather to add to my picture. Something silver glistened in the sand. I rushed over, but it was only the pop-top from an aluminum can. I stuck it in my pocket so nobody would step on it with bare feet and get cut.

I added the new stones and feathers to my sea picture, then aimed my camera at it and adjusted the focus. Just as I snapped the shutter, a pair of shoes jumped into the middle of my picture, kicking the feathers, stones, and shells into a jumbled pile.

"Hey!" I said. I let the camera dangle from its strap around my neck. "What'd you do that for?"

Daren stood inside my former picture, smirking at me. "Do what?" he asked.

"You wrecked my picture."

"No, I didn't."

I stared at him. How could he deny it when the evidence was right there under his feet?

Daren ground a feather into the sand with his heel. "You ran off and left me stuck in the elevator."

"I didn't run off. I told the hotel clerk you were stuck, and he said he'd call the repair service."

"Right," Daren said, as if he didn't believe me. He dragged one foot back and forth, erasing the remains of my picture frame.

"How'd you get here so fast?" I asked. "The repairman must have already been in the building."

"The elevator started working again by itself. It was only stuck a couple of minutes. When I got to the lobby I saw you through the big window walking toward the beach, so I followed you."

I put my camera back in the carrying case and turned away from Daren.

"Where are you going?"

I pointed. "My parents are over there. I'm sup-posed to meet them."

"That was a stupid picture you made in the sand," Daren said.

In my head I said, *It was a really great picture, and you're stupid for wrecking it.* Out loud, I said nothing.

So much for my summer goals.

I'm a coward, I thought as I walked away. A wimp. A big baby who's scared to stand up for himself.

I'll probably never learn to pop a wheelie either, and I'll strike out every time I get up to bat, and Mom and Dad will be so disgusted with me they'll cut my allowance in half.

When I got to where Mom and Dad were sit-ting, Mom said, "I saw you talking to Daren. Do you want to invite him to come to our room with you and BeeBee while we're gone this evening? His parents will be going on the cruise with us. He could eat with you and . . ."

"No!" I said. It came out louder than I meant it to.

Mom cocked her head sideways and waited for me to explain.

"I don't like Daren too much," I said.

"Why not?" Mom asked.

"He smokes." That was true. Twice I'd seen him light a cigarette as soon as he got off the school bus. I thought Daren was dumb for smoking, but it was not the reason I didn't like him. However, I knew Mom wouldn't want me to hang out with a kid who smokes.

"He's mean," BeeBee said. "He picks on kids at school all the time."

"Does he pick on you?" Dad asked.

"No," BeeBee said.

"If he ever does, you tell him to knock it off or you'll report him to the principal," Dad said. "You can't let bullies get away with being mean or they'll come back for more."

I braced myself, fearing Mom would jump into the conversation with a million questions, but for once she didn't.

She nodded at Dad's advice to BeeBee and said no more about Daren.

That afternoon, when it was time for Mom and Dad to leave, I got even more instructions than usual.

"You can charge the pizza to our room," Dad said, "but tip the delivery person with cash." He gave me a five dollar bill.

"They get five dollars just for bringing a pizza to us?" BeeBee asked.

"Yes," Dad said, "and don't get any funny ideas about only giving him part of it and keeping the rest."

"Maybe I won't be president of a bank when I grow up," BeeBee said. "Maybe I'll deliver pizza instead."

"You'd have to carry a lot of pizza to earn as much as a bank president makes," Mom said. "Not everyone gives a big tip."

I was tempted to ask about a tip for the baby-sitter but decided not to push my luck. Tomorrow, after I reported how smoothly our evening had gone, I would ask again about an increase in my allowance.

"You can watch TV while we're gone," Mom said, "or any of the G-rated movies or play cards or read. But stay in our room. We don't want you wandering around outside without us."

"Can I watch *Money Talk* at seven o'clock?" BeeBee asked. She looked at me since she knows I don't like that program.

"Sure," I said. "I'll write my postcards to Gary and Grandpa and Grandma while you watch it."

"We'll have the cell phone with us," Mom said, "but I don't know if there's reception on the ship. Probably not."

"Kyle is not going to call us and interrupt the Salesman of the Year program," Dad said. "We'll be clear out on the ocean, anyway. If there's a problem, he can call the front desk."

"We'll be fine," I said. "It's no different than when we stay at home, so don't worry about us."

Mom gave me a hug. "Thanks," she said.

"Have a good time," I said. After they left I put the chain on the door in case Daren decided to pay us an unannounced visit.

BeeBee and I played gin rummy for awhile. Then we read the room service menu and chose what kind of pizza we wanted. Even though it was only five o'clock, we decided to eat. "Let's order milkshakes too," BeeBee said. "I want vanilla."

"Sounds good to me."

I had never ordered anything from room service but it was easy. "Charge it to Room 303," I said, as if I charged things every day of my life.

"While we wait for the food to come," BeeBee said, "let's buy candy bars from the machine. They can be our dessert."

"We ordered milkshakes," I said. "I don't want a candy bar too."

"I do. I'll eat it later while I watch *Money Talk*."

"We're supposed to stay in the room."

"Mom and Dad let me use the candy machine last night. It's down the hall, just past the elevator."

I decided a trip to the candy machine wasn't the same as wandering around alone, so I said yes. I let her go by herself in case Mom called. She often calls when BeeBee and I are alone, and I knew she would freak out completely if she called the room and nobody answered.

"Go straight to the candy machine and come right back," I said.

"You sound like Dad," BeeBee said. She scooped three quarters from the pile of change Dad had left on the dresser top, picked up Bill, and skipped down the hall.

I stood in the doorway and watched her pass the elevator and turn the corner to the alcove where the candy machine was located.

Before she came back, the phone rang.

"Hi, honey," Mom said. "We're getting ready to board the ship and wanted to be sure everything's okay with you guys."

"We're fine," I said. "We ordered pizza and milkshakes, and we're waiting for them to be delivered."

"Oh, good. We'll see you later then. Love you."

"Love you too."

I hung up and went back to the doorway. BeeBee should have been back by now.

The hallway was empty.

4

"BeeBee?"

No reply.

I put the room key in my pocket, closed the door, and headed for the candy machine. A sign taped to the front of it said, "Out of order. Use machine on second floor."

I frowned, annoyed at my sister. She knew she shouldn't go downstairs by herself. I walked back to the elevator and looked up at the arrow. It was partway between two and three; she must be on her way back up. When the doors didn't open, I looked again. The arrow still pointed between floors.

Oh, great! BeeBee was stuck in the elevator. I waited a minute, hoping the elevator would start again by itself, the way it had when Daren got stuck, but the arrow didn't budge.

I returned to the room and called the front desk. "The elevator is stuck again," I told the clerk.

"Is anyone on it?"

"Yes. At least, I think so; I'm not positive."

The clerk sighed loudly into the receiver. "We have to pay the repair service double time after five o'clock," he said. "Unless we know there's someone stuck between floors, we'll wait until tomorrow morning to call them."

"I'll make sure my sister isn't on the stairs," I said.

I raced down the hall to the stairway, galloped down to the second floor, and checked the candy machine there. No BeeBee. I ran back upstairs. I glanced at the elevator arrow before I returned to the room; it was exactly where it had been the last time I looked at it.

I unlocked our room and called the front desk again.

"The elevator's still stuck," I said, "and my sister's on it." *She had better be,* I thought, *because if she isn't, where is she?*

I stood in the doorway where I could see the elevator and still hear the phone if it rang. I knew my parents wouldn't call again, but the man at the desk might call to tell me when the repairman would arrive.

I'm in charge, I thought. I should never have let her out of my sight. I should have gone with her. If nobody had answered the phone when Mom called, she would have called again in a few minutes.

My stomach felt knotted up like a pretzel. I was almost certain BeeBee was stuck on the elevator, but I remembered news stories about kidnapped children. One minute a child was with his parents in a shopping mall or a bowling alley or some other public place, and the next minute the child had vanished. Many times I had seen TV clips of weeping parents pleading with whoever had taken their son or daughter to bring that child back. I knew how Mom and Dad would react if they got back to the hotel tonight and learned that BeeBee had disappeared.

No. I pushed the shocking scene out of my mind, refusing to let my imagination take that path. She's on the elevator, I told myself. She has to be!

I wiped the palms of my hands on my jeans and wondered how long it usually took for the repair service to arrive. I wouldn't let myself think about what would happen if the elevator got fixed but BeeBee wasn't on it.

The stairway door opened. A man carrying a cardboard pizza box and a white paper bag came down the hall. The man's face was red; beads of sweat dotted his brow.

"You ordered a pizza?" he asked. The words came out in wispy puffs as the man tried to catch his breath.

"Yes. Thanks." I took the box and the bag and set them on the table in the room.

The man followed me into the room. He took a handkerchief from his pocket and patted his forehead with it. "It's bad enough we have to deliver clear over here from the Frontier Lodge kitchen," he said, "but I had to walk all the way up to the third floor. The elevator's broken."

"I know. Thanks for bringing our order." I handed the man the five-dollar bill.

He looked less grumpy as he tucked the bill in his pocket. "Thank you, sir," he said.

BeeBee appeared in the doorway.

Relief and anger mixed in my mind like two colors of paint swirling together. "You're in big trouble," I said.

"The elevator got stuck, but it's working again," BeeBee said as she came into the room. She didn't look at me, but directed her words to the pizza man.

"I needed it more coming up," he said. He left, closing the door behind him.

"What were you thinking?" I demanded.

"The candy machine on this floor didn't work."

"You knew you shouldn't go downstairs alone. You should have come and told me, and I would have gone with you."

At least she had the sense to look guilty. "I did come back to get you," she said, "and I heard the phone ring. I knew you were talking to Mom and I thought I could go get my candy bar and be back before you hung up. I would have made it too, if the elevator hadn't stopped."

"You scared me half to death. I didn't know if you were on the elevator or if some nutcase had abducted you."

BeeBee hung her head.

"It happens, you know," I said. "Practically every week there's a report on the news about some kid who disappears."

"I didn't think about that," BeeBee said.

"You didn't think, period. You could have been chopped in pieces and stuffed in the Dumpster."

BeeBee's lower lip quivered, a sure sign that tears would soon flow. "Are you going to tell Mom and Dad?"

"Maybe." I knew I wouldn't tell them because I was somewhat to blame for what had happened. I should have gone with her to the candy machine instead of letting her go alone. But I didn't tell BeeBee that. I wanted her to worry about her possible punishment for awhile. That way, she wouldn't pull a stupid stunt like this again.

"Where's your candy bar?" I asked. "Don't tell me the other machine was broken too."

"I ate it while I sat in the elevator." She grinned at me. "Dessert first," she said.

"Let's eat our pizza before it gets cold," I said. I opened the box. The pizza smelled delicious. Pineapple, tomatoes, and extra cheese—my favorite kind. I handed BeeBee a napkin.

"Thank you, sir," BeeBee said, sounding exactly like the delivery man.

I smiled. It was hard to stay mad now that everything had turned out okay.

"How does it feel to be a big spender?" BeeBee asked.

I took a bite and ignored her. As I set my slice of pizza down, the table tilted. One side lifted up while the other side went down. The carton of pizza slid off the edge, flipped, and landed cheese-side down on the floor. The milkshakes would have gone too, if we hadn't grabbed them.

At the same time, the chairs we were sitting

on seemed to sink and then come up again, like one of the rides at the county fair.

"Whoa!" BeeBee said. "Did you feel that?"

A lamp toppled off the bedside table.

We let go of the milkshakes and clung to the arms of the chairs as they dipped down again.

"It's an earthquake!" I said, my heart thudding like a bass drum. I felt frozen in place, my shocked brain incapable of thought.

"My milkshake spilled," BeeBee said. "It's all over the rug."

The whole room swayed from side to side; pieces of the bathroom ceiling crashed to the tile floor.

Everything that was on top of the dresser tumbled off. Sunglasses, Mom's hairbrush, the postcards I'd bought, the envelope with our tickets for the flight back to Kansas City, and Dad's pile of change all landed in a heap.

BeeBee leaned down to look under the table. "The pizza's wrecked," she said. "It's all dirty." She started to pick it up. As she did, her chair moved again, causing her to bump her head on the table. "Ouch!" she yelped.

Somehow her cry brought me to my senses. I needed to keep us from getting hurt, if I could.

"Get on the floor," I said, "and cover your head

with your hands." I hoped I didn't sound as scared as I felt.

We crouched with our foreheads on the floor and our arms over our heads. The old green shag carpet smelled musty and I saw stains that I hadn't noticed before. Two peanuts, dropped by a former occupant of the room, hid under the desk.

I heard a crackling sound, like static on the radio, followed by a "Poof!" that seemed to come from the roof. The lights went out.

Enough daylight came through the window that I could see around the room. Everything moved. It was as if the entire building had been placed in a large box and now a giant was shaking the box. The drapes swung back and forth; BeeBee's bucket of stones tipped over, dumping the contents; Dad's shaving kit slid off the bathroom counter and crashed to the floor on top of the broken pieces of ceiling.

Beside me, the bed creaked as if someone was bouncing on it.

Bang! A loud noise exploded outside, behind the hotel.

"Was that a gun?" BeeBee asked.

"I don't think so. Maybe a big tree fell down."

We had hunched side by side with our hands on

our heads for only a minute or two, but it seemed like hours. Then, as suddenly as it had started, the shaking stopped. BeeBee put her hands down and began crawling toward her spilled stones.

"Don't get up yet," I said. "There may be after-shocks."

"The rug stinks. I don't like putting my face by it."

"Sit up then, but keep your hands over your head in case any more of the ceiling comes down."

We remained on the floor for a few minutes more but nothing else happened.

"I guess it's over," I said.

I got up, stepped over the milkshake puddle, and walked to the window. BeeBee stood beside me. Everything outside looked exactly as it had before. Down on the beach the waves licked against the shore, and far out on the water a large yacht was silhouetted against the sky. I wondered if it was the *Elegant Empress*. Had Mom and Dad felt the earthquake out on the ocean? Or was the water so deep that it cushioned the jolts that came from the earth far below?

"Wow!" BeeBee said. "That was exciting! Wait till Mom and Dad hear we had an earthquake while they were gone." She began picking up her stones and putting them back in the bucket. "Can we order another pizza and more milkshakes?" she asked. "Maybe the hotel won't charge us to replace them since it wasn't our fault they spilled."

I didn't reply. All I could think about was the sign we'd seen at the beach that morning. I couldn't remember exactly how it was worded, but I did remember that as soon as an earthquake ended we were supposed to run away from the water and go as far inland and as high uphill as we could go.

Mom and Dad had told us to stay in the hotel while they were gone—but this morning Dad had made sure we understood the warning sign's instructions.

So, should BeeBee and I stay where we were, or leave the hotel and hike up the hill?

5

If everyone was supposed to leave the hotel and go to higher ground, wouldn't an alarm go off? Maybe not inside an old hotel like this, but outside somewhere? There must be some sort of warning signal to let people know.

Back home, whenever a tornado approaches, sirens sound all over town. When we hear the tornado sirens, we all head for the nearest building and go down to the basement until the "all clear" signal sounds.

BeeBee laid a bath towel on the spilled milkshakes. "Yuck," she said. "What a mess. When you call room service, ask for a maid too."

I tried to remember what Gary had said in his report last year about a system that tracked tsunamis, but I couldn't remember the details. Besides, his report had been on Hawaii. He hadn't mentioned Oregon.

"Do you smell something funny?" BeeBee asked.

I sniffed. "Like what?"

"Burned toast."

I sniffed again. She was right; something smelled scorched.

"Probably when the electricity went out, a transformer blew up or something," I said. "Maybe that's the bang we heard that sounded like a gunshot."

I reached for the phone.

"I want a chocolate milkshake this time," BeeBee said.

"I'm not calling room service. I'm calling the front desk to report the smell." I also planned to ask about a warning signal for tsunamis, and if the clerk didn't know, I would try to call Mom and Dad on the cell phone. Maybe the cell phone *did* work on the ship. I knew they wouldn't mind having me call in an emergency like this to ask what we should do.

I held the receiver to my ear and pushed the button for the front desk. Nothing happened. I jiggled the button up and down. There was no response and no dial tone. The line was dead.

BeeBee pointed the remote at the television set and pushed the clicker several times.

"The power's off," I said. "There's no TV and no telephone."

"It had better get fixed before *Money Talk*," she complained. "I want to watch my program."

"Put your shoes on," I said, trying to keep my voice calm. "We're going to go outside and get farther away from the ocean."

"Mom and Dad said we're supposed to stay in the room."

"They didn't know we were going to have an earthquake."

"The earthquake's over. I don't want to go outside. We didn't eat yet, and I want to order another pizza and a chocolate milkshake."

I wondered how she thought the cooks were supposed to bake pizza without electricity. My sister might be smart about money, but she wasn't using her head now.

"Remember the sign we saw at the beach?" I said. "The one about tsunamis?"

"Yeesss," she said, drawing out the word while she soaked in the meaning of my question.

"We're going to do what the sign said."

BeeBee looked at me as if she'd never seen me before. "Is a giant wave coming here?" she asked.

"I don't know. Probably not. But in case a big wave does come, we need to get as far away from the ocean as we can."

BeeBee slid her feet into her sneakers, grabbed Bill, and followed me to the door.

I unhooked the door chain, but when I tried to open the door, it didn't budge.

"Is it locked?" BeeBee asked.

"No, it's stuck. The earthquake must have shifted the building."

BeeBee started to cry. "I want to go outside!" she wailed. I was too worried to point out that two minutes earlier she had insisted she wanted to stay in the room.

I turned the doorknob again, then put one foot on the wall to brace myself while I yanked with all my strength. The door jerked open about six inches—and a thick cloud of dark smoke billowed into the room.

I slammed the door shut again.

"That's what I smelled," BeeBee said. "There's smoke in the hallway."

Beep . . . beep . . . beep. I jumped as the shrill sound filled the room.

BeeBee covered her ears. "What's that noise?"

Beep . . . beep . . . beep. Was that the tsunami warning? No, it was too close; a tsunami warning would come from outside the hotel; this was coming from overhead. I looked at the ceiling and saw the source of the racket: a round piece of plastic that was mounted over one of the beds.

"It's a smoke alarm," I said.

"Make it stop," BeeBee said. "It hurts my ears."

"We aren't staying here," I said. I ran to the bathroom, turned on the faucet, and soaked two bath towels with water. I handed a dripping towel to BeeBee. "Hold this over your nose and mouth," I said. "We're going into the hall to find the stairs and go down."

"I don't want to," BeeBee said. "I want to stay here. The hall is full of smoke."

Beep . . . beep . . . beep. The clamor continued.

I hesitated. Maybe we were safer here in the room with the door closed. But something was burning enough to fill the hall with smoke. There was a fire somewhere in the hotel; the whole building could eventually go up in flames.

I didn't want to be trapped in our room on the third floor. What if we had to jump out a window? Even if we only made it down one flight of stairs, we'd have a better chance of leaping to safety from a second-story window than from the third floor.

"Hold the towel over your face," I said, "and hang on to me."

She dropped Bill and buried her nose and mouth in the wet towel.

I tugged on the door again, pulling it open far enough for us to squeeze through. I held my own towel with my right hand and grabbed BeeBee with my left.

"Let's go," I said.

With no lights and no windows, the hall was as dark as an underground cave. Thick smoke surrounded us. Even with the towel held to my face, my eyes smarted, and the smoke stung the inside of my nose when I inhaled. I coughed, and BeeBee's cough echoed mine. Luckily, we knew where the stairway was and went in that direction.

I wondered if there were people in any of the other rooms. We had not seen anyone except the Hazeltons on the third floor, but that didn't mean the rooms were empty. If we hadn't opened our door, we wouldn't have known there was a fire. What if other unsuspecting guests were in their rooms?

"Hang on to my shirt," I said. I dropped her hand and pounded on the doors of the rooms we passed. "Fire!" I shouted. "Leave the building! Fire!" I coughed and put the towel back against my face, trying not to take a deep breath.

BeeBee stumbled along beside me, one hand clinging to my shirt. "Can't we take the elevator down?" she asked.

"With the electricity out, the elevator won't be working." Even if it had been running, I wouldn't take a chance on that old elevator.

We had to be nearly to the stairwell. I groped along the wall, feeling for the door.

My foot landed on something soft. I stumbled and fell against the wall. BeeBee couldn't catch herself in time and went down.

Wondering what I had tripped over, I leaned down and extended one hand. My fingers landed on a face. I jerked away just as BeeBee screamed.

"There's a body on the floor!" she cried as she scrambled to her feet. "It's a dead person!" She flung her arms around me and buried her face in my chest.

I pushed her away, then dropped to my knees and gingerly put my fingers down again. I felt hair—short, sharp spikes of hair. I'd seen only one person in the hotel with that kind of hairdo. "It's Daren Hazelton," I said.

"Is he dead?"

I moved my fingers across Daren's face and under his chin, feeling for a pulse. When I felt a steady throbbing, I blew my breath out in relief.

"He's alive," I told BeeBee. "He must have been overcome by the smoke."

I shook Daren's shoulders. "Daren! Wake up!"

He groaned but didn't move.

"Daren, it's Kyle," I said. "Wake up! You have to get out of here."

"I found the door to the stairs," BeeBee said. "We're right next to it."

"Hold it open while I move Daren into the stairwell."

I heard a slight creaking as the door opened.

"It isn't as smoky on the stairway," BeeBee said.

I put my hands under Daren's armpits and dragged him through the doorway onto the landing.

"Shut the door," I said. "Quick! Before any more smoke comes through."

BeeBee did. We still couldn't see but at least it was easier to breathe.

"What are you going to do about Daren?" BeeBee asked.

I hesitated. I wasn't sure I should pull Daren down two flights of stairs. What if he had injured his neck or back when he fell to the floor? If I moved him the wrong way, he could be permanently paralyzed. But I couldn't leave him behind in a burning building either, and besides, I'd already moved him.

"We're going to take him with us."

"He's too big to carry."

"I'll pull him behind me, like a wagon."

"We'll get out a lot faster if we leave him here."

"The whole building might go up in flames. We have to try to save him."

"I don't like Daren."

"I don't like him either, but we can't leave him here unconscious."

"If we were unconscious," BeeBee said, "I bet Daren wouldn't rescue us."

I knew she was probably right about that. I also knew it would be wrong to save ourselves and leave Daren behind, no matter how much I disliked him.

"You go down first," I said. "Hang on to the railing and keep the towel over your nose and mouth. I'll be right behind you."

"What about your towel? You can't hold it over your nose and pull Daren at the same time."

"I'll have to do without the towel."

"Bend down," BeeBee said. "I'll tie it around your face, like a bandit." She managed to secure the towel behind my head, and it stayed in place when I leaned over to grab Daren's shoulders. I put one hand under each of Daren's armpits and lifted so that his head wouldn't touch the steps. Walking backward, I started down, towing Daren after me.

It was like dragging a huge rag doll down the stairs. Daren's feet made a soft *thunk, thunk* sound as they slid from step to step. His arms dangled at his sides, and I couldn't believe how heavy he was. It took every bit of strength I had to keep going. If I'd had to pull him *up* the stairs, I would never have made it.

The stairs went down half a flight to a landing, where they doubled back and went down some more. Coughing, I paused on the landing to catch my breath. The landing was hard to navigate since we had to change directions.

"Hold Daren's head for me," I instructed BeeBee, "while I move his feet."

BeeBee kept Daren from sliding headfirst down the stairs, while I lifted his feet and swung them around the landing so that we could proceed. It was slow going, and I wasn't sure I should be taking this much time. What if I saved Daren but in doing so, cost BeeBee and me our lives?

Sweat dripped off my forehead; my shirt clung to my back. As we crossed the second-floor landing and started down another section of stairs, the smoke got thicker. Ahead of me, I heard BeeBee coughing and choking.

"Try not to inhale the smoke," I said. "Keep the

towel pressed against your noise and take shallow breaths."

"Hey!" The sudden voice made me jump. "What's going on? Where am I? Let go of me!" Daren pushed my hands away.

I couldn't see him, but it sounded as if he rolled onto his side and then sat on one of the steps.

"We're in the stairwell," I said. "We're taking you downstairs with us because the hotel's on fire."

"What are you trying to do, break every bone in my body?"

"You had passed out up on the third floor," I said.

"No, I didn't."

"We found you lying on the floor next to the elevator."

"I didn't pass out."

I saw no reason why he would contradict the truth, but I wasn't going to stand there and argue with him while the hotel burned down around us. With both of us coughing in between words, breath was too precious to waste.

The acrid smell was stronger now. It smelled like hot plastic or rubber mixed with some other odor that I didn't recognize. With my hands free again, I pressed the wet towel closer to my nose and mouth with my left hand and took hold of the handrail with my right.

"It stinks in here," Daren said.

"It's the smoke. I told you: There's a fire in the hotel. We're almost to the ground floor. Can you walk by yourself now?"

"Fire!" Daren said as if he had finally come to and understood for the first time what was happening. He scrambled to his feet, lunged past me, and shoved BeeBee aside as he went by her. She lost her footing and fell, landing on her knees two steps down.

"I have to get out of here!" Daren cried, panic making his voice squeak. "The hotel's on fire!"

I helped BeeBee up. "Are you okay?" I asked.

"I told you we should have left him behind," BeeBee said.

6

Now that I didn't have to drag Daren behind me, BeeBee and I moved quickly down the remaining stairs. As we rounded the last landing, we saw a bright flash of light below us.

Daren had opened the door from the stairway to the lobby.

"Help!" he shouted. "Somebody help me!"

We hurried down the last few steps toward the door, but before we got there, the light disappeared; Daren had left the stairwell, letting the door close behind him.

My brain raced even faster than my feet. I knew the electricity was still off; if it had come back on, the lights in the stairway would be working. So the flash of light that we saw when Daren opened the door to the lobby could mean only one thing: The first floor of the hotel was on fire.

Could we run through it and get outside? Or

should we go back up to the second floor, try to find an unlocked room, open a window, and yell for help?

What if all the rooms were locked? Even if we got to a window and called for help, who would hear us? As far as I knew, the desk clerk was the only staff person on the premises; everyone else, like the bellhop and the room service man, came over as needed from the new Frontier Lodge. Better to take our chances crossing the lobby now, before the fire got any worse.

We reached the bottom of the stairs. I put my hand on the doorknob but didn't turn it.

"The main floor is on fire, isn't it?" BeeBee said.

"I think so."

In my mind, I pictured the hotel lobby. "As soon as I open this door," I said, "run straight ahead. Just to the right of the front desk, there's a door that goes outside. It's closer to the stairway than the main entrance is. I went that way this morning when I came back to the room for my camera."

I took a deep breath. "Ready?" I asked.

"Ready."

I pulled the door open, felt a blast of hot air, and saw why Daren had called for help. The entire lobby was ablaze. The area where the front desk had been was an enormous bonfire with fingers of flame reaching toward the ceiling.

The carpet looked as if someone had set dozens of tiny fires in a random pattern across the floor. Sparks flew up, then drifted down again, like flocks of fireflies.

The plate glass window overlooking the Pacific Ocean had shattered, and the sea breeze blew in, fanning the flames.

"Run!" I yelled. I grabbed BeeBee's hand and took off, lifting my feet as high as I could, trying to avoid the burning patches of carpet. I felt as if I were in a war zone, dodging land mines. I expected the floor beneath us to ignite into solid flames at any second.

At least I could see. After the dark stairway, the fire in the lobby was so bright that I had to shut my eyes partway, but I saw the outside door that I remembered, and I led BeeBee toward it.

I grabbed the brass door handle, then jerked my hand back. The smell of blistered, charred skin joined the smell of smoke as the pain shot up my arm. I ripped the wet towel from my face and used it to open the door.

I pushed BeeBee through first, then stumbled after her.

I heard sirens now, rising and falling like a pack of howling wolves. Fire trucks must be on the way.

We ran away from the burning building. When we were far enough to feel safe, we stopped and looked around. I expected to see other hotel guests or employees who had escaped, but I saw no one. BeeBee and I might have been the only people in the world.

I wondered where Daren was. Had he made it out, or was he still trapped in the burning lobby? If he had headed for the main lobby doors rather than the small side door that we had used, he may not have reached it. I wished he had stayed with us instead of pushing ahead by himself. Well, I wasn't going to go back to look for him when I didn't know if he was inside.

My hand throbbed where I had burned it on the door handle. I pressed the wet towel against the burn.

BeeBee began to cry.

"We're safe now," I told her.

"I know," she said, her voice trembling, "but I left Bill upstairs in the room."

"Maybe he'll be okay. Hear the sirens? The fire trucks should be here any second."

"Do you think Daren got out?"

"I don't know. I hope so."

"You saved his life," BeeBee said, "and he didn't even wait for us."

"Shh. Are those sirens still getting louder?"

"Yes. No. They were coming closer, but now they've stopped."

We heard people shouting.

"I see our room," BeeBee said, pointing up. "Top floor, right over the lobby."

I looked. Yellow flames shot out of every window on the third floor. As we looked up at our room, the roof collapsed with a loud rumble like a dozen dump trucks all unloading at the same time. For a second I thought it was another earthquake; then I saw that the Totem Pole Inn was caving in on itself. The fire roared skyward as the flames consumed the roof beams.

I shuddered, thinking what would have happened if we had stayed in our room or on the second floor.

"Bill is burning up," BeeBee said.

"I'm sorry," I said, and I meant it. BeeBee had carried Bill Bear around with her for so long that he really seemed like one of the family. I let her cry for a few seconds. Then I said, "Come on."

"Where are we going?"

"We'll walk around to the back of the hotel," I said, "to the road. Then we're going to go up the hill."

BeeBee didn't argue. She slipped her hand in mine and together we skirted the remains of the burning Totem Pole Inn.

The odd smell I'd noticed inside was stronger now, making my head ache.

"I smell gas," BeeBee said.

When we reached the road behind the hotel, the voices were louder. We saw more flames across the street.

"Look!" I said. "The new hotel's on fire too."

"There are the fire engines," BeeBee said. "That's why the sirens stopped; the firefighters came to the Frontier Lodge."

From where we stood, the road ran downhill to the Frontier Lodge. The dark smoke from the two fires blew inland, giving us a good view of the burning lodge.

"I hope the owners had insurance," BeeBee said.

Although the sun hadn't set yet, the sky had an orange glow. I peered nervously at the waves washing onto the beach below us. They were the same size as always.

I looked toward the horizon, trying to see the

yacht that Mom and Dad were on, but it was no longer visible. Either it had gone beyond my view, or it had already come home.

I hoped the *Elegant Empress* had returned early, and that Mom and Dad were on their way back to the Totem Pole Inn. I liked baby-sitting when nothing went wrong. Ordering pizza and tipping the delivery man had been fun—but being in charge during an earthquake and a fire wasn't fun at all. It was terrifying.

"There you are!" Daren came up behind us. His clothes looked singed, and he was missing one shoe.

I never thought I'd be glad to see Daren Hazelton, but it was a relief to know he had made it out of the hotel. Even so, I tensed, expecting him to slug me.

For once he kept his hands to himself.

"Are you hurt?" I asked. "Did you get burned?"

"One sneaker caught fire, and I had to kick it off, and after I got outside I coughed up a lot of black gook, but I'm okay. What about you?"

"I burned my hand on the door handle when we left the lobby."

"I stepped out through the broken window." He said it as if he had been far more clever than I had been. "What are you standing here for?"

"We're watching the fire," BeeBee said.

"We aren't staying here," I said. "We're going up the road, to the top of the hill."

"Are you crazy?" Daren said. "Look at all the trees on that hill. I hiked up there this morning and it's nothing but woods. With both hotels on fire, those woods will probably catch fire too. There'll be a huge forest fire, and if you go that way, you'll be trapped in it."

"Where are you going to go?" BeeBee asked.

"After I watch the fire, I'll go down to the ocean. Water won't burn, so the beach is the safest place to be."

"What if there's a tsunami?" I said.

"A what?"

"A tidal wave. Sometimes earthquakes trigger tsunamis, and a sign on the beach said it could happen here. When there's an earthquake, everyone is supposed to go uphill as soon as the earthquake ends. Get as far away from the water as possible."

"I don't plan to be burned alive in a forest fire and I'm not scared of getting washed away by a wave," Daren said.

"Suit yourself," I said. "BeeBee and I are climbing the hill."

We left Daren and followed the road up the hill.

Daren called after us. "If you have a brain in that thick skull of yours, Davidson, you'll go down to the water with me instead of running away from nothing like a scared rabbit."

If no tsunami comes, I thought, *I'll never hear the end of this. Daren will tell every kid at Edison School that I ran away while he was brave.*

7

"What if he's right?" BeeBee asked. "What if we go in the woods and then they catch fire?"

I glanced over my shoulder. Daren still stood in the road near the Frontier Lodge watching the fire.

"The firefighters are already battling the blaze," I said. "I don't think it will get out of control."

"They're only fighting one fire," BeeBee said. "What about the Totem Pole Inn?"

"Maybe they'll let it burn," I said, "since it was going to get torn down soon, anyway. Officially, the inn is closed. The firefighters may not know anyone was staying there. They won't let the fire spread to the trees, though."

We continued up the road. I wasn't sure that this was the right choice. The sign had said a tsunami could follow an earthquake within a few minutes. It had been at least fifteen or twenty minutes since the earthquake. Did that mean there was no danger of a tsunami? If so, we might be safer at the beach or near the hotel, where other people were.

Daren's theory about the fire spreading made sense, and as far as I knew no tsunami warning had been issued. Of course, if there *was* a warning in effect, I wouldn't know it.

My mind went in circles like Alexander the Greatest when he chases his tail. One second I thought we should hurry up the hill; the next second I wondered if we should return to the hotel area.

The thing that kept me going uphill was my memory of Dad's voice saying, "You got that?" after he had read the sign to us. Mom and Dad trusted me to take care of BeeBee and myself. By doing what the sign said to do, I hoped I was keeping us safe.

BeeBee trudged at my heels. "I'm tired," she said, "and hungry. I want my pizza and my milkshake."

"I don't think room service delivers out here," I said.

BeeBee didn't laugh. "I want Bill." Her voice quavered as if she were going to start crying again.

I felt like crying myself. Besides losing Bill, we had lost all of our clothes and our luggage and our plane tickets home. BeeBee hadn't thought of any of those things yet, and I didn't intend to tell her. I could imagine the moaning I'd hear once she realized her new sun hat was gone and the bucket of shells and her favorite pajamas that had dollar signs all over them.

Now that we were away from the burning Totem Pole Inn, the road was more narrow. Ruts and potholes made it hard to walk without looking down all the time. The farther we got from the ocean, the more the smoke hung in the air. My eyes smarted. I kept blinking, but it didn't help much.

"Why isn't anyone else going this way?" BeeBee asked.

I had wondered that myself and didn't know the answer.

"Maybe there are wild animals around here," BeeBee said.

"Wild animals fear fire," I said. "They'd run away even faster than we can."

That seemed to satisfy her.

We had walked another five minutes, when a concrete barrier blocked our way. A small sign beside it said: "No vehicles beyond this point."

We walked around the barrier and found that the pavement had ended. We were now on a dirt path that headed up at a much steeper incline than before.

My hand throbbed where I had burned it on the door handle, and my throat hurt from all the smoke.

I stopped walking long enough to wipe my face on the bottom of my shirt.

"Do you hear that?" BeeBee said.

I listened. Somewhere in the distance I heard, "Moo. Moo. Moo."

"It's cows!" BeeBee said.

"Is that the kind of wild animal you were worried about?"

"I meant cougars or grizzly bears. I hear a whole herd of cows."

I knew that animals sometimes sense a natural disaster ahead of time. I'd read about dogs and cats back home in Kansas who pace nervously around before a tornado strikes. One woman in our town had a parrot who, she claimed, knew a tornado was headed in its direction long before the weather service issued any warning. Were the cows aware that another earthquake was coming? Or a tidal wave?

We stood still for a moment, straining to hear better. The mooing repeated, over and over and over, sounding exactly the same each time.

"I don't think those are live cows," I said.

BeeBee giggled. "Dead cows don't moo."

"I think it's a recording."

She listened again. "You're right. Why would anyone play a tape of cows mooing?"

We walked on.

"The farmers make a tape of their cows mooing," I said, "and then if one of the cows doesn't come home at night with the others, the farmer plays the tape over a loudspeaker, and the stray cow hears it and knows where to go."

"Is that true," BeeBee asked, "or are you making it up?"

"Making it up," I admitted, "but it's logical. I can't think of any other reason why someone would broadcast a bunch of cows."

"That mooing noise is coming from the direction of town," BeeBee said. "There weren't any cows in town."

While we pondered the puzzle, we heard voices on the road behind us. Looking back, we saw a man and a woman go around the concrete barrier and hurry toward us. The woman had a small tan terrier on a leash.

"Hello!" the man called when they were a bit closer. The little dog wagged her tail and tugged toward us.

"Hello," I said.

"Keep going up the hill," the woman said. "There's been a tsunami warning! It's supposed to hit Fisher Beach at five-thirty."

"We aren't supposed to go anywhere with strangers," BeeBee whispered to me.

"This is an emergency," I whispered back, "and we aren't going with them; we were climbing the hill anyway."

"Hurry!" the man said as they caught up to us.

"They look like Grandma and Grandpa," BeeBee whispered.

I nodded, and we fell into step behind the gray-haired couple and their little dog. I felt less anxious now that we were near adults, strangers or not.

The dog kept turning around, wanting to sniff us. "Come along, Pansy," the woman said. "You can make friends after we're out of danger."

"How did you know about the tsunami?" I asked. "Was there a warning on the radio?"

"We heard the cows mooing," the man said.

"We heard them too," I said. "It sounded like a tape recording."

"That's the tsunami warning," the man said. "The town council decided cows wouldn't be as frightening as a siren, so when there's a tsunami warning in this area, they broadcast the sound of cows mooing."

"In Kansas we have tornado warnings," BeeBee said, "but the warnings don't sound like cows; they're sirens. We didn't know what the mooing meant."

"That's a problem," the man said. "We knew because we live here, but visitors don't have any idea what it means when those cows start in. Of course, they might not know what any other warning signal means either."

"We thought a farmer had lost one of his cows and was calling it home," BeeBee said.

"Oh, lawsy, that's a good one," the woman said.

"If there's been an official warning, why aren't more people coming up the hill?" I asked.

"Usually guests from the Totem Pole Inn come up the hill with us, but the inn isn't open any more," she said. "I heard two or three rooms were used last night because of a convention, but officially it's closed. The new lodge isn't renting rooms yet, so only a small staff is on duty. With the fires and all, they may have left before the tsunami warning."

"We stayed at the Totem Pole Inn last night," I said.

"I'm glad you got out safely," the man said. "We're the ones who called the fire department. We live in a beach cabin just down the road."

"Do you have neighbors?" BeeBee asked. I knew she was still wondering why other people weren't coming up the hill with us.

"None close by," the man said. "There are always a few people having beach picnics this time of night, but many of the locals ignore the warnings because there have been so many false alarms. The cows moo, the radio and TV announcers get all excited and create a panic, and when the wave finally comes, it's only two feet high. It's happened half a dozen times."

"The problem," the woman said, "is that the scientific weather instruments can predict the time of a tsunami, but not the size of the waves."

"Warning signals only work if people trust them," the man said. "I'm afraid the folks who live around here have lost their trust."

"We told those people watching the hotel fire to get to high ground," the woman said, "but most of them went down to the beach instead. One girl said if there was a tidal wave, she wanted to see it. I told her, 'Honey, the only way you'll see a tidal wave is when it washes you away,' but she laughed and went down to the water anyway."

"Has a tsunami ever hit this area?" I asked.

"Not in the fifteen years we've lived here, but the experts keep saying it's going to happen, so every time there's a warning we take Pansy for a walk up the hill. Better safe than sorry, that's my motto. By the way, I'm Josie and this is Norm."

"I'm Kyle," I said, "and this is my sister, BeeBee." It would have seemed like an ordinary conversation, except that all of us kept walking as fast as we could, as if we were hurrying to catch a bus.

"Kyle's a hero," BeeBee said. "He got us out of the hotel when it was on fire, and he rescued a boy who had passed out from the smoke, only that boy wouldn't come up here with us. He said it was safer at the ocean because water doesn't burn."

"Maybe he'll hear about the tsunami warning," Norm said. "Sometimes officials go around and broadcast the news. They tell people to evacuate, to go to higher ground."

"Where are your parents?" Josie asked.

"They went on a cruise," BeeBee said. "They're having dinner on a big yacht."

I added, "It's a business event for the company they work for. They had to go because our dad was the salesman of the year, but the dinner was only for adults." I didn't want this couple to think Mom and Dad were a couple of deadbeats, off at a party while their kids were left alone in the hotel. "We ordered pizza from room service, and then we were supposed to watch a movie until they got home."

"The pizza fell on the floor and the milkshakes spilled," BeeBee said.

My throat felt tight. Talking about Mom and Dad made me wonder again where they were. If they were still out on the ocean, what would happen if a tsunami hit? Would the ship be able to ride the huge wave, or would it capsize?

If the ship had headed back early because of the earthquake and the fires, the captain would know about the tsunami warning and would tell the passengers where to go to stay safe. But would Mom and Dad do it, or would they rush to the Totem Pole Inn looking for us?

Now that I knew there was an official tsunami warning, I was certain I'd done the right thing by coming up the hill, but I also realized how much danger my whole family was in.

BeeBee apparently had the same thought, for she said softly, "What if Mom and Dad get washed away by the giant wave? What if we never see them again?"

I didn't answer. I couldn't reassure my sister when I was every bit as worried as she was.

8

The celebration on board the *Elegant Empress* was in full swing. Cotton ball clouds drifted across the sky, and the hum of the ship's engine accompanied a string quartet that played soft music in the background.

The Davidsons filled their plates at the buffet table.

"You can win salesman of the year anytime," Mrs. Davidson told her husband, "if it means an evening like this."

"It *is* special," he agreed, "but don't expect me to win every year. Enjoy it while you can."

"I feel guilty being on a yacht eating grilled vegetables and salmon and chocolate mousse while the kids have pizza in that dumpy hotel room."

"Now don't start worrying about the kids," Mr. Davidson said. "BeeBee seems to like having Kyle be the sitter, and I don't think he minds too much.

Besides, they'd rather eat pizza than grilled veggies any day." He helped himself to some garlic bread.

Just then Mr. Wray, the president of the real estate company, signaled to the quartet to stop playing. He went to the microphone and said, "Ladies and gentlemen, I'm sorry to interrupt your dinner, but the captain has received a radio message that the town of Fisher and Fisher Beach were hit by an earthquake a short time ago."

Mrs. Davidson gasped and reached for her husband's hand.

"There wasn't any major damage, and as far as we know there were no injuries, but the power is out in the entire area and we have reports of a few fires that started when the earthquake broke a natural gas line."

Mrs. Davidson opened her purse and removed the cell phone. Mr. Davidson took a piece of paper out of his pocket and handed it to her. On it was the phone number of the Totem Pole Inn.

She punched in the number and waited. "Nothing happens," she said. "It doesn't ring."

"If the power is out, the hotel's telephone line is probably out too."

"I'll keep you posted on any further developments," Mr. Wray said. "Now please enjoy the rest of your dinner. We'll be presenting the awards soon."

Instead of returning to their table, the Davidsons approached Mr. Wray.

"Shouldn't the *Elegant Empress* head back to shore?" Mr. Davidson asked.

"The earthquake is over," Mr. Wray said. "There's no reason to go back early."

"We left our children at the hotel," Mr. Davidson said, "and the phone isn't working. Is there any way we can contact the hotel by radio?"

"I'll ask the captain," Mr. Wray said, but he looked annoyed.

"You stay here and finish your dinner," Mr. Davidson said. "I'll find the captain."

"I'll come with you," Mrs. Davidson said.

They left their food at their places, then found the captain and asked about radio contact with people on shore. "We left our children by themselves," Mrs. Davidson explained. "Our son's thirteen and he's stayed with his sister many times before, but never in an earthquake. We'll enjoy the rest of the cruise more if we know they're okay."

"Which hotel?" the captain asked.

"The Totem Pole Inn."

A strange expression flickered across the captain's face.

"What is it?" Mr. Davidson said. "What's wrong?"

"That's one of the buildings that caught fire. That and the big new hotel right beside it. I understood that the Totem Pole Inn was closed. I didn't realize people were staying there."

"We have to go back to Fisher Beach," Mr. Davidson said. "Now! Our kids might be hurt or in danger."

"I have radio contact with shore," the captain said. "I'll see what I can learn and then . . ."

"Excuse me, sir." One of the crew approached the captain. "There's a tsunami warning for the Fisher Beach area."

"When?"

"It's due to hit in half an hour."

Mrs. Davidson whispered, "No."

Mr. Davidson turned pale.

"We won't be able to return as scheduled, sir," the crewman said. "Should we stay here or head out to sea?"

"Out to sea."

"We can't head farther out to sea!" Mr. Davidson said.

"I'm responsible for the passengers on this ship," the captain said, "and the farther out we are, the safer they'll be. Excuse me." He hurried away and disappeared into a room marked "Crew Only."

Mr. Davidson turned to the crewman. "Our children are at Fisher Beach, and the hotel they're in is on fire! We have to get back there right away. Is there a small boat or life raft that we can use?"

The crewman shook his head. "That would be foolhardy," he said. "You'd risk your own lives, and even if you made it, there's no way you would get to the hotel in time. We're too far out at sea. The town broadcasts tsunami warnings; your kids will be told what to do."

"We should never have left them alone," Mrs. Davidson said.

"The tsunamis usually peter out before they reach shore," the crewman said. "There's never been damage on this part of the coast. We've had many warnings, and then the waves turned out to be so small we couldn't tell when they passed under the ship. That will probably happen again."

"Thank you for telling us," Mrs. Davidson said. "I hope it's a small wave this time too."

The crewman left, and the Davidsons stood alone on deck as the music drifted out of the banquet area.

"We may as well go back to our table," Mr. Davidson said.

"I've lost my appetite."

"So have I, but I don't want to miss anything that the captain tells the group."

They walked back to the party.

"We should tell the Hazeltons about the fire," Mrs. Davidson said. "As far as I know, their son was in the hotel too."

"It would only worry them. They can't go there or do anything to help their boy any more than we can help Kyle and BeeBee."

"Still, I would want to know," Mrs. Davidson said.

They spotted the Hazeltons across the room and were headed that way when the captain made an announcement about the tsunami warning. "We're heading due west," he said, "to ride the waves before they gain their full size. I expect the ship to handle any surges easily, but all passengers need to put on a life jacket and leave it on until the danger is past."

Mrs. Hazelton screamed and demanded that the ship head for shore immediately. "My baby's at Fisher Beach," she sobbed. "My baby!"

Mr. Hazelton threatened to sue the real estate company if anything happened to Daren.

Mr. Wray did his best to calm them down, but the Hazeltons continued to create a scene long after the captain hurried out of the room.

Mr. and Mrs. Davidson put on life jackets and sat praying silently for the safety of their children.

After Kyle and BeeBee left him, Daren watched the firefighters at the Frontier Lodge. Huge streams of water arced from thick hoses, making the fire hiss and spit like an angry cat.

A dozen people milled around, talking about where they had been during the earthquake. Everyone had a story to tell.

Daren listened but said nothing. He didn't want anyone to know that he had been overcome by smoke and rescued by that wimpy Kyle Davidson. If Kyle ever told what had happened, Daren would deny it.

Daren wondered if his parents were still on the yacht. Did they know about the earthquake and the fires? If they did, they'd be plenty worried about him.

He had wanted to go swimming or walk on the beach after they left, but Mom and Dad insisted it wasn't safe for him to do those things by himself. He was supposed to stay in their room at the Totem Pole Inn until they returned. Period. No excuses.

Ha! Daren thought. It's a good thing he hadn't

done that. If he had stayed in the room, he'd be a goner.

When his parents got back and discovered that the Totem Pole Inn had burned to the ground, they'd be sorry they had told him to stay in the room. Maybe he would let them look for him for a while before he showed them he was okay.

It was fun to be out here alone, with all the excitement of a fire and nobody to boss him around. Along with the shouts of the firefighters, he heard the snapping of burning wood and, somewhere in the distance, the mooing of cows.

A van with an official seal on the door drove into the hotel driveway and stopped behind the fire truck. Large megaphones anchored to the roof of the van blared out: "ATTENTION! A TSUNAMI WARNING HAS BEEN ISSUED FOR THE FISHER BEACH AREA. FOR YOUR OWN SAFETY, GO TO HIGHER GROUND IMMEDIATELY. REPEAT: A TSUNAMI IS EXPECTED TO HIT FISHER BEACH AT FIVE-THIRTY P.M. GO TO HIGHER GROUND NOW AND STAY THERE UNTIL YOU'RE NOTIFIED THAT IT'S SAFE TO RETURN."

Daren looked at his watch: It was already five-twenty. The tsunami would be here in ten minutes!

He scowled. Kyle had said he was going up the hill because there might be a tsunami. Daren didn't want to be wrong and have Kyle be right. He had been so sure that Kyle was foolish to run away. Now the van made it sound as if the beach might be dangerous, as Kyle had said.

Daren glanced around, wondering if all the other people who were watching the fire would heed the warning and run for higher ground.

Nearby, a group of teenagers began debating what to do. "I'm going to stay right here," one girl said. "If a big wave hits the beach, I'll be able to see it from here, but we're far enough back to be safe."

Two women hurried past.

"You won't be safe here," one woman said to the teens. "You need to get as far from the beach as you can. Everyone does."

The two women got into a pickup truck at the edge of the parking area, started the engine, and drove off toward the town of Fisher.

The girl called after them: "Send me a postcard!" Her friends laughed.

Daren laughed along with the teenagers, but his laughter felt forced. What if those women were right? It was embarrassing enough that Kyle had found him unconsciousness in the hallway; it would be even worse if Kyle was safe on top of the hill while Daren got hit by a big wave at the beach.

He turned to the man standing next to him, who wore a bellhop uniform from the Frontier Lodge.

"Are you going to go up the hill?" Daren asked.

"Not me," the man said. "I've heard that song too many times before."

"What do you mean?"

"The government is always coming around with tsunami warnings that scare away the tourists. People get hysterical, check out of the hotels, and leave town. They don't come back even though the tsunami never hits. I'm tired of the whole thing. It's bad for business."

If anyone should know about possible danger, Daren thought, *it was the bellhop who worked here every day.*

"If it was really risky to be here," the bellhop continued, "those men wouldn't be driving around in their van scaring people; they'd be racing uphill to save themselves. This is just another false alarm. It happens all the time."

A woman standing nearby spoke up. "I worked at the Totem Pole Inn for ten years and my mother worked there before me. In all that time, it never got hit by any tidal wave."

Daren smiled. So Kyle was wrong after all. Good.

He decided to go down to the water's edge. If he

saw a big wave approaching, he could always run away then. Even if the wave caught up to him, he was a strong swimmer. He'd be okay, and tomorrow he could tease Kyle about being a scaredy-cat who ran away from a foot-high wave. Daren liked that idea.

He looked at his watch again. Five-twenty-four. Only six minutes until the tidal wave was supposed to arrive. Daren turned away from the smoking hotel and hurried down the wooden stairs that led to the beach.

Someone had started a small driftwood bonfire. Four people stood near it, gazing out toward the water. Two others gathered more wood and tossed it on the flames.

Their voices buzzed with excitement as they took turns calling out the exact time.

"Five-twenty-five!"

Daren walked past the bonfire and stood as close to the water as he could without getting his feet wet. He felt daring, and brave.

"Five-twenty-six!"

What a day! Daren had never had so many exciting things happen. He had been in an earthquake and a hotel fire, and now he was standing at the edge of the ocean during a tsunami warning.

He looked toward the horizon. None of the approaching waves seemed any higher than the waves that had splashed the shore all day. The bellhop was right. The officials were frightening people for no reason.

The sun was a red basketball as it slid toward the horizon.

Tiny white lights twinkled far out to sea. Daren wondered if the lights were from the *Elegant Empress*.

"Five-twenty-seven!" the voices shouted.

Daren kicked off his sneaker and waded into the water. He wished Kyle could see him now. When they talked about this tomorrow, Daren would make Kyle look like a baby.

Someone shouted from the top of the wooden steps: "Hey! You people on the beach! There's a killer wave coming! Get away from the water now!"

Daren froze. Killer wave sounded a lot worse than tsunami. What if he wasn't being brave by staying in the water? What if he was being stupid?

Kyle and BeeBee were not here now; they wouldn't know whether Daren stayed or ran. He could still brag tomorrow that he had waded in the water while they ran away.

The shout came again: "Run, you fools! A killer wave's almost here!"

Daren bolted away from the water. Two of the people who had been watching the bonfire ran after him, ignoring the jeers of their companions.

Daren took the steps two at a time. He reached the top and was racing toward the burning Totem Pole Inn when he heard the voices on the beach yell, "Five-thirty!" A cheer rose from around the bonfire.

Daren kept running.

9

"I need to rest," BeeBee said. "I have a crick in my side."

"We're almost to the top of the hill, honey," Norm said, "and it's nearly five-thirty. Keep going just a little longer."

"We made it this far," I told BeeBee. "Let's try to reach the top before five-thirty. Then we can sit down until it's safe to go back."

"My feet hurt," BeeBee said. "I burned my ankle when we crossed the lobby."

"We'll soon be there," Josie said. "I see the park bench where we always wait."

I saw a sturdy bench ahead, the kind with iron legs and wooden slats for the seat and back. When we reached the bench, Norm and Josie sank down on it, clearly worn out from the long climb. Pansy sniffed the grass beneath the bench.

"This is as high up as we can get," Norm said.

"We could keep walking farther inland, but there's no path—just trees and undergrowth that would be hard to get through, so we always sit here and wait until we hear the 'all clear' signal."

Josie scooted over close to Norm. "There's room for all of us on the bench, if you don't mind being cozy."

BeeBee sat on the bench beside Josie. When Josie draped her arm around BeeBee's shoulders, BeeBee rested her head against the woman's plump figure.

"I'll sit in the grass," I said. I dropped to my knees, then stretched out on my back. Instantly, a wet tongue began licking my face.

"Pansy!" Josie said. "Leave that boy alone."

"Puppy kisses! Puppy kisses!" BeeBee said.

"Pansy loves kids," Norm said. "Twice she dug under our fence and ran off; both times she went straight to the school yard down the street to play with the kids. We finally extended the fencing a foot down into the dirt so she can't get out, but she loves it if kids stop and talk to her when they walk past."

I petted the coarse tan fur with my left hand. I still had the towel wrapped around my burned right hand and I wasn't in any hurry to take it off. "You're a good dog," I said. "Good Pansy."

"Someone has made a bonfire on the beach," Norm said.

I sat up and looked. Far below, a small circle of light flickered against the dark sand, not far from the water's edge. Clumps of people stood near it, looking like miniature action figures. I wondered if one of them was Daren.

"I can see the hotels too," BeeBee said. "The Totem Pole Inn is still burning, but the fire is nearly out at the new lodge."

I gazed down at the remains of the two buildings.

"I suppose you lost your clothes," Josie said, "and your luggage."

"Yes," I said.

"I lost Bill," BeeBee said. "He burned up." Her lower lip quivered and tears trickled down her cheeks.

"Bill was her teddy bear," I explained.

"Now don't you cry, honey," Josie said. "Here, use my handkerchief. It's my favorite one."

BeeBee took the handkerchief and mopped her face.

"When your parents get back," Josie said, "we'll take them and you to our place for the night. We have two extra beds and you kids can have sleeping bags on the screened porch. It'll be much better than trying to find a hotel room."

"Cheaper too," Norm added. "No charge."

"Cheap is good," BeeBee said.

"We can lend you pajamas and clean clothes for tomorrow," Josie said. "I have an apple pie in the freezer. Won't take long to heat that up."

"Don't we still have Arnie's old bear?" Norm said. "Maybe BeeBee would like to have that."

"Arnie's our son," Josie said. "He has kids of his own now, but he never wanted to keep any of his childhood toys. Yes, I believe the bear is packed in that box in the spare bedroom and in need of a child to love him."

"That's nice of you," BeeBee said. "Thank you."

I could tell BeeBee was relaxing, comfortable with this kindly couple. I was glad to be with them too, but I couldn't stop thinking about the tsunami warning. Was it a good idea to wait here, or should we be running farther inland? Just because there had been false alarms in the past didn't mean that's what would happen this time.

I wished Mom and Dad were on top of the hill with us instead of—instead of where? I assumed they were still aboard the *Elegant Empress* but I didn't know that for sure.

"What time is it?" I asked.

"Five twenty-eight," Norm said. "If there's a big wave coming, it'll be here soon."

"Do you know what happens to ships when a tsunami strikes?" I asked.

"I heard about some fishermen," Norm said, "in Japan, I think it was. They were out to sea when a tsunami went right under their boats and they never felt it. Didn't know anything had happened until they returned home and found their village in ruins."

"That's right," Josie said. "So don't be worrying too much about your mom and dad. They're probably safer out on the water than anywhere else."

A happy shout went up from the people near the bonfire, then died away. It sounded like a crowd at a football stadium.

Norm looked at his watch and shook his head. "Those blockheads on the beach are cheering because it's five-thirty," he said.

I kept one arm around Pansy as I looked down toward the water.

Norm and Josie didn't speak again. Even the dog sat still, as if she knew we were waiting and listening for something important.

"What does the 'all clear' signal sound like?" BeeBee asked. "Horses neighing?"

Norm guffawed, and Josie laughed until she had to wipe tears from her cheeks.

"It's a *beep, beep* sound, like the noise big trucks make when they're backing up," Norm said. "But I'll suggest the horses to the town council. They're so fond of the cows, they'll probably take your suggestion."

We were still chuckling when Pansy started barking. "Woof! Woof! Woof!"

"What's Pansy barking at?" Josie asked.

"That's her warning bark," Norm said, "the kind she makes when someone comes to our door."

Pansy began to tremble, shaking as if she were scared silly.

"What's wrong, girl?" Norm asked. "We aren't at the vet's office." He patted Pansy but she continued to shake.

That's when we heard the big wave.

A roaring noise like a dozen low-flying airplanes came toward us from the west. We jumped to our feet and looked down toward the ocean.

About a hundred yards from shore, the surface of the water lifted up, rising higher and higher as it approached land. I'd watched TV programs of surfers riding big waves, but this one was ten times higher than any I'd ever seen.

The wave spread sideways as far as I could see. It was not only going to hit Fisher Beach, but also all the shoreline on both sides of the bay.

"Look at that!" Norm said.

It was gigantic and it moved unbelievably fast. There was no point in us running into the woods now; the wave traveled far more swiftly than we could.

The people on the beach who had cheered just moments earlier, now turned away from the water and ran for their lives. The bonfire disappeared. The fleeing people were swallowed up before they ever reached the wooden steps that led to the hotels.

I could see the crest of the wave below us and knew it was not high enough to reach our vantage point. I also knew that if BeeBee and I had not come to the top of the hill, we would have been washed away along with the unfortunate people below us. I swallowed hard, blinking back tears.

We watched the wall of water rise over the top of the hotels, then curl back into itself and crash down on the back side of the burning buildings. In two seconds the giant wave did what the firefighters had tried to do for twenty minutes. The flames sputtered and died under the huge volume of sea water that poured down on top of the hotels.

The four of us stood at the top of the hill, staring down at the incredible wreckage as the wave slid back where it had come from, taking with it pieces of the two buildings and the people who had been near them. A yellow fire engine bobbed upside down on the receding wave, its tires spinning in the air.

My eyes darted back and forth, looking for survivors. Far from shore, a person straddled a piece of lumber, riding it like a horse. I saw objects in the water but couldn't tell if they were people swimming or bodies floating or merely items that had been washed out to sea.

The Totem Pole Inn was a heap of rubble except for the concrete tower that housed the elevator shaft. Two people lay on the flat roof of the tower, apparently carried there by the wave.

Frontier Lodge, blackened from the fire, still stood, but there was now a big boulder where the front door used to be and an uprooted tree leaned crazily off the corner of the roof.

Norm's voice brought me out of my shock. "We can't stay here," he said. "We must go farther inland. Quickly!"

Josie took BeeBee's hand. "He's right," she said. "That wave missed us, but the next one might be higher."

"I'll carry Pansy," Norm said. He scooped the little dog up and tucked her under one arm. "Let's go!" he said.

Neither BeeBee nor I said a word. If there were waves even bigger than the one that had just hit, we didn't want to be anywhere near them. We turned inland and took off.

This time we didn't walk as we had going up the hill. We ran. We crashed through the underbrush like startled deer as we followed Norm and Josie into the woods.

In my mind I replayed the horrible scene we had witnessed below us. The people on the beach were gone; I was sure of that. How could they not be? There were twenty-seven wooden steps that led from the beach to the Totem Pole Inn, and a couple more steps up to the road in front of Frontier Lodge. That wave had risen not only over all the steps, but over the tops of the two hotels! I shuddered, imagining the force of so much water.

The firefighters had been pulled into the sea too, along with anyone who had lingered to watch the fires. If the wave had hit the town of Fisher as hard as it had hit this inlet, the whole town was probably destroyed.

BeeBee must have been thinking the same

thoughts because she said, "Do you think everyone on the beach drowned?"

"Most of them probably did. I saw one person who had climbed on a driftwood log or something and stayed afloat."

"Maybe that was Daren."

My stomach lurched when I thought of Daren. I was glad I hadn't eaten the pizza and drank the milkshake because if I had, I'd have lost them both.

As I plunged through the scrub brush, I remembered Daren jumping into my sea picture and wrecking it. I remembered him shoving past us in the stairway when he realized the hotel was on fire. I remembered how it felt when he punched me in school—day after day, year after year. Most of all, I remembered his cocky voice saying he'd be safer at the beach than we would be "running away from nothing" up the hill.

I thought about my list of summer goals.

Oh, Daren, I thought. *I wanted to stop your bullying—but I didn't want it to happen this way. I didn't want you to die!*

I looked back but could no longer see the ocean or the horizon in the distance. The trees were thick now, mixed groves of tall Douglas fir, alder, cedar, and others that I couldn't identify. The undergrowth was thicker too, with prickly vines that grabbed at my pant legs. Fallen branches, rocks, and mounds of decomposing leaves made the ground uneven.

We stumbled often but managed to stay upright as we fled. My legs ached from lifting my knees so high with each step. I'd been running at the high school track all spring and summer to help me increase my speed in baseball, but it's much easier to go fast on a smooth surface than it is to move through dense undergrowth in a forest.

With all the smoke in the air, dusk arrived early, giving the woods a forbidding look.

Josie stopped running so suddenly that I almost bumped into her. "My legs can't carry me one step farther in these bushes," she said, her breath coming in gasps. "I'm going to sit here on this big rock and wait."

"Then I'll wait with you," Norm said. "You kids take our flashlights and keep going. It'll be pitch dark soon." He and Josie both held flashlights out to us.

"I want to stay with you," BeeBee said.

"Your legs are younger than ours, honey," Josie said.

"You're healthy and strong; you can keep running. Go as far as you can."

"We'll take one light," I said. "You keep the other one."

"Good luck," Norm said. "Now go!"

"Thank you," I said as I took Norm's flashlight. "Thank you for everything."

BeeBee and I ran on, not knowing what was ahead of us and not caring. All I cared about was putting as much distance as I could between us and the next giant wave.

Before, when I had made the decision to come up the hill, I had known that a tsunami had terrible destructive power, but now I had seen that force with my own eyes. Fear that comes from personal experience is far more real than fear based on someone else's ordeal.

As darkness wrapped around us, we slowed down some. I wasn't sure how far inland we'd run. Half a mile? Maybe even a mile.

When I ran laps around the track at school, I always set a goal and then counted the laps. Knowing there were only three more to go, then two more, then one, made it easier to finish even when I was so tired I didn't think I could make it.

I wished I could count down now. How much

longer did we need to run? How far would be far enough? The woods stretched on, seemingly forever.

Beside me I heard BeeBee panting and wondered how long she would last. My own legs were so tired that I was having trouble running through the undergrowth now, and her legs were shorter than mine.

"Are you okay?" I asked.

"I can't run much more. I wish we could have stayed with Josie and Norm."

"It's safer to keep going."

"My feet hurt and my arms are all scratched up."

Her words started as a sentence and turned into a whine. I knew if I encouraged her to talk any more she'd soon be in tears.

BeeBee rarely cries at home unless she's overtired. Now she was not only weary but also scared and in danger. I didn't blame her for being weepy; I felt like crying myself.

"Shh," I said. "We'll stop for a few seconds to catch our breath and listen. Maybe we'll hear the signal that it's safe to go back."

"What if we hear another wave coming?"

"Then we'll run some more."

The darkness surrounded us now, and although the pool of light from the flashlight made it possible to keep going without bumping into a tree, it also made me feel more vulnerable. We couldn't see beyond the light—but anything in the woods nearby could see us.

We stood in the middle of nowhere, listening to the darkness. I didn't hear any all-clear signal, but even if it was sounding, I wasn't sure it would carry this far. We were a long way from Fisher Beach now and even farther from the town of Fisher, and there were huge trees to mute the sound. I didn't know if the town still existed, anyway. Maybe the speakers that broadcast the warnings and the all-clears had already been washed away by the first big wave. Maybe the people who monitored tsunamis were gone.

I listened some more. I didn't hear the all-clear signal, but I didn't hear another wave approaching either.

What I did hear were twigs snapping and brush breaking as someone—or something—came through the trees toward us.

BeeBee clutched my arm. "Something's coming!"

"Hello!" I called. "Who's there?"

The noise came closer.

I couldn't see the source of the noise.

BeeBee inched around until she stood behind me, then peeked over my shoulder.

I kept the flashlight pointed toward the noise.

Two bright eyes glowed in the gloom.

10

"Is it a grizzly bear?" BeeBee asked.

"No. It's too short." It was too short to be a human too, but I didn't say that.

What else lived in the woods? A mountain lion's eyes would be about that high. So would a coyote's. Maybe it was a bear cub, and the mother bear was right behind it, ready to protect her baby.

I swallowed hard. I would wait until the animal was close enough so I could tell what it was. Then I planned to clap my hands and shout and try to scare it away.

Another twig snapped.

The eyes advanced.

My light picked up a tuft of tan fur and two floppy ears.

"Pansy?" I said.

The little terrier gave a happy "Yip!"

"It's Pansy!" BeeBee said. "Here, Pansy!"

Giddy with relief, I laughed as Pansy ran toward us, jumping over the low-lying bushes, snapping twigs.

"Pansy!" BeeBee dropped to her knees and hugged the dog. Pansy slurped BeeBee's face as her tail whipped back and forth.

"She must have pulled the leash out of Josie's hand and run after us," BeeBee said.

"I can't believe she would leave Norm and Josie."

"Norm said she loves kids. Maybe she just wanted to be with us."

I shined the light back and forth in the woods where Pansy had come from, thinking Norm and Josie would follow Pansy and try to catch her. "Norm!" I called. "Josie?"

There was no answer. Maybe Josie truly couldn't walk any farther.

"We need to go on," I told BeeBee. "We've rested long enough."

"We can't keep running now! We can't leave Pansy by herself."

"Pansy'll come with us. If she has trouble getting through the bushes, I'll carry her the way Norm did."

"I want to hold her leash."

That's when I realized that Pansy's red leash was

not dangling from her collar. "The leash is gone," I said.

Maybe Norm and Josie had purposely let Pansy come after us so that she would be farther away if another tsunami hit. Maybe they were hoping to save their little dog whether they were safe themselves or not.

I felt bad for Norm and Josie, knowing they would be worried about Pansy. They'd been so kind to us; I wished I had a way to let them know that Pansy had found us, and that we would take care of her and bring her back when the danger was over. That is, we'd bring her back *if* we survived.

We went deeper into the trees. I felt as if I were having a nightmare—the kind where I know I'm in danger and it's imperative to run way, but I can't seem to make my legs work.

I wished I had paid more attention to the maps of the Oregon coast that Dad had shown us when we were planning this trip. In particular, I wondered what lay straight east of Fisher Beach. If we were running away from the ocean—and I hoped we were still going in that direction, although I knew it was possible that by now we were disoriented and going around in circles—I wished I knew what was ahead of us. Would we eventually come to a road? A town? Farms? Or did these lonely woods go on for miles?

Pansy stopped.

"Come, Pansy," BeeBee said. "This way."

The terrier, who moments before had willingly trotted alongside us, now stood stiff-legged, refusing to budge.

"Is she hurt?" I asked. "Is her paw caught in a bramble?"

I shined the light on Pansy. The dog was shaking with fear. "It's okay, Pansy," I said.

"Woof!"

The sharp bark made me jump—and sent a shiver of premonition up my back. Did Pansy sense something that I couldn't yet know?

"Woof! Woof! Woof!" It was the same bark Pansy had given just before the tsunami hit.

"Another wave is coming," BeeBee said.

I swung the flashlight in a circle, looking for a safe place to wait. We were near a large tree, a giant old-growth cedar. I ran to the tree and put both arms straight out sideways; the tree trunk went from the fingertips of one hand to the fingertips of the other.

"Come here," I said. "We're going to stand on the far side of this big tree. If another wave comes, the tree will protect us."

It was a sturdy shield, but would it really be strong enough to protect us from a tsunami?

BeeBee followed me to the back side of the tree.

"Stand as close to it as you can," I said. "Press up against the bark."

BeeBee stepped up on a large root that angled away from the bottom of the tree and leaned her forehead against the trunk.

I turned off the light and put it in my pocket, then gathered the terrified dog in my arms and stood directly behind BeeBee. I felt BeeBee's shoulders shake and knew she was crying.

"Turn around," I said. "Put your back against the tree, and face me. We're going to make a dog sandwich."

BeeBee turned, wiping her nose on the back of one hand. "Dog sandwich?"

"You and I are the bread, and Pansy's the filling in the middle," I said.

BeeBee put her arms around Pansy. "Good dog," she whispered. "You're a good, good dog."

Pansy's tail swished against me as she licked the tears from BeeBee's cheeks.

I wondered how I could make up a silly joke about a dog sandwich when I feared we were going to die any minute. Still, my words had helped.

BeeBee wasn't crying any more, and now that we were holding her close, Pansy had stopped shaking.

If disaster strikes, I thought, *I've spent my last few minutes on Earth hugging a dog and calming my sister's fear.* Those are good things—but I didn't want these to be my last minutes on Earth. I didn't want to die making a dog sandwich or running through the woods or any other way. I wanted to live! I wanted to survive the tsunami and find Mom and Dad and go back home to Kansas. I wanted to play baseball and hang out with my friends and read some good books and ride my scooter and . . .

I heard what Pansy must have heard a few minutes earlier.

"Here it comes," BeeBee said.

We huddled behind the tree and listened to the second giant wave roar toward us. I could tell from the sound that it was higher than the first one had been and coming farther inland.

Pansy began to tremble again.

"It's coming over the top of the hill!" BeeBee shouted.

I tightened my hold on Pansy and pushed even closer to BeeBee.

I heard trees crash to the ground, and for one awful moment I feared I had made a terrible mistake by staying behind the big cedar tree. What if the force of the water pushed the tree over on top of us, trapping us beneath it?

Well, it was too late to change my mind. The fastest runner in the world wouldn't be able to escape the wave when it was this close.

The water thundered forward. I ducked my head down, shielding BeeBee, and braced my legs to keep my balance.

"It's going to hit us!" BeeBee screamed.

We should have run inland sooner, I thought. Instead of staying with Norm and Josie and watching the people on the beach with their bonfire, we should have kept going. We should have run as far and as fast as we could. The warning sign had said to go as high up and as far away from the water as possible. Why had I followed only half the instructions?

Small stones, propelled forward by the water, hit our tree, then bounced to the ground like hailstones.

I closed my eyes.

Pansy whimpered.

BeeBee pulled me even closer.

The wave splashed to Earth just before it reached us. It must have crested over the treetops, because now I heard water smashing down on the woods we had run through minutes before.

The ground shook as the water poured down. I heard crashes and loud thuds. Something more than trees was being dropped by the wave. Rocks? Pieces of driftwood? Charred timbers from the hotels? It was too dark to see what the wave carried; all I could do was hope that none of it landed on us.

Water rose around our ankles, then quickly receded. Once the wave hit, it reversed course and hurried back to where it had begun.

As the wave rushed away from us, we stayed where we were, fearing a third wave would follow.

"That was close," I said.

"Too close," BeeBee said.

I shifted Pansy to a different position. For such a small dog, she sure got heavy in a hurry.

"How many giant waves will there be?" BeeBee asked.

I tried to remember Gary's report. Had he talked about a third or fourth wave sometimes being the worst one? I couldn't recall, and I wished BeeBee would quit asking questions as if I were somehow an authority. I wasn't the expert. I was just a kid who no longer wanted to be responsible for his sister.

"I don't know," I said. "If the worst is yet to

come, we should keep running." I stepped out from behind the tree.

BeeBee did too. "Thank you, tree," she said.

"Thank you, Pansy," I said. If she hadn't alerted us that another wave was coming, we wouldn't have made it behind the tree in time.

I tried to put Pansy down but she whimpered so pathetically that I continued to hold her even though my arms ached. I turned on the flashlight and moved it slowly back and forth.

"Everything's changed," BeeBee said.

The woods we had walked through now looked as if loggers had chopped down trees at random and left them leaning haphazardly against each other.

Much of the low undergrowth had washed away; what was left wore a thick layer of sand. A twisted piece of metal the size of a car's bumper glinted in my light; I couldn't tell what the metal had been, but I knew if it had come down on a person, it would have inflicted serious injury.

The ground was littered with beach chairs, broken bicycles, and other odd pieces of man-made items that had been lifted by the water and transplanted here.

I stopped my light on a large rectangular piece of

wood that stuck out of the ground at an angle, one corner of it jammed into the dirt.

"It's a sign," BeeBee said as she walked closer to it. "It's the big sign from the front of the Totem Pole Inn!"

The foot-high carved letters and the life-size totem faces were black from the fire. The sign had been mounted on two tall logs the size of telephone poles near the front door of our hotel. I thought of the power necessary to rip that heavy sign free and carry it over the top of the hill.

"I wonder if Norm and Josie are okay," BeeBee said.

I was afraid they weren't, since the wave had landed right where they had been, but I didn't say that. I didn't even want to think it.

I couldn't hold Pansy any longer. I set her down. The dog sniffed the sign, then rolled in the wet sand. Her fur was a mess, but it didn't matter. She was alive. That's all that mattered for Pansy, and for BeeBee and me. We were alive.

I cupped my hands around my mouth and shouted, "Norm! Josie! Can you hear me?"

My words floated away like soap bubbles.

"We'd better keep going," I said.

"No. I can't run any more. I'm worn out."

"There might be another wave, even bigger than the last one."

"I don't care," BeeBee said. "I'm too tired to run anymore; I need to rest." Her face was pale, her arms were scratched from running through the woods, and I knew she wouldn't make it much farther no matter how desperate our situation.

My burned hand throbbed, my head ached, and my legs felt like rubber. BeeBee was right; we both needed to rest.

"I don't have the energy to keep running either," I said. "If another wave comes this far, we'll stand behind our big tree again and hope for the best."

"Good. I'm going to sit right here and wait for Mom and Dad to find us." She plopped down on the trunk of a downed tree.

I sat beside her. I doubted that anyone would find us, but if no more waves came, we could wait here until daylight. By then surely it would be safe to return to Fisher Beach.

I wondered what was left of Fisher Beach and the town of Fisher. Had the small village survived? Was anyone there to broadcast an all-clear signal when it was safe to return?

Where were Mom and Dad? Was the *Elegant Empress* unharmed somewhere out at sea—or had the tsunami waves destroyed it?

What had happened to Norm and Josie?

My mind overflowed with questions, but I didn't know how to find any of the answers.

11

Each minute seemed like an hour.

We sat on the fallen tree, listening for another giant wave. I kept the flashlight off, saving the batteries in case we needed to see.

My mind was as weary as my body. The fire, the fear of a tsunami, and my worry about Mom and Dad had drained me of energy as much as climbing the hill and running through the woods had.

Tired as I was, I worried that we shouldn't stay where we were; we ought to keep going. When we first got to the top of the hill, we should have kept running rather than sitting on the bench. That decision had probably been fatal for Norm and Josie. Now we were sitting again instead of running farther inland. Was I making the same mistake twice?

With so many trees down, the next wave would have less resistance. It might travel faster and farther.

I fretted and stewed over the possibility, but I didn't move. BeeBee and I were exhausted. If a bigger wave came now we wouldn't be able to outrun it anyway.

I had done my best to save us. Now I sat in the dark, and waited.

The only sound was Pansy's gentle snoring.

BeeBee's head kept drooping down, then jerking back up, the way it does when she falls asleep in the car.

"Let's sit on the ground," I said, "and lean back against the tree."

We sat in the damp sand.

"My clothes are getting dirty," BeeBee said, "and my shoes are all wet. Mom won't like that."

"It's okay. Mom will be so glad to see us, she won't care how dirty we are."

"I wonder if Daren drowned," BeeBee said.

"He should have come with us."

"I'm glad he didn't."

The anger in her voice surprised me.

"I didn't tell Mom and Dad the truth about Daren," BeeBee went on.

"What do you mean?"

"He hits me. At school he sneaks up behind me during recess and pushes me. Sometimes he pokes me with a pencil, and if I cry, he calls me a baby."

Outrage exploded inside me. I was far more furious at Daren for bullying BeeBee than I had ever been over getting hit myself. I wondered if Daren had picked on BeeBee because she was my sister. That possibility made me feel sick.

"I never told on him because I was scared he'd do something worse to get even."

Remorse settled on me like a quilt; I felt its weight on my shoulders.

"I know this is a terrible thing to say," BeeBee continued, "but if Daren doesn't come back, I won't miss him."

I wouldn't miss him either, but I hoped he was alive. If I never saw Daren again I would always regret letting him get away with hassling me for so long. I should have taken a stand with Daren years ago. If I hadn't wanted to confront him myself, I should have talked to a teacher or my parents about the problem.

I had always been afraid to tell him off, for the same reason BeeBee hadn't told a teacher. I feared Daren would get angry and beat up on me. Now I saw that there are worse things in this life than getting thrashed, and one of them is feeling shame for not having the courage to do what's right.

I wished with all my heart that I had stood up to Daren when he wrecked my sea picture. With my parents in shouting distance, it had been the perfect chance to tell him to knock it off, but I hadn't done it. Now I might never be able to, and I would always regret acting like a coward.

I'm not a coward, I thought. *I saved us from the fire, and so far we've survived the tsunami because of me. Daren's the one who panicked on the hotel stairs, not me.*

Why did I ever let him bully me? If I had stopped him years ago when his bullying first began, he might never have picked on BeeBee at all.

"If Daren escapes from the tsunami," I vowed, "I'll see that he never bothers you again."

"I thought you were scared of him too."

"I used to be, but I'm not anymore."

BeeBee thought about that for a minute. Then she said, "If Mom and Dad don't come back, what will happen to us?"

I'd already thought about that, and I knew the answer. "We'll live with Grandma and Grandpa," I said. "They'd move to a bigger house so they could take us."

"Good." BeeBee laid her head in my lap and promptly fell asleep.

Pansy draped her muzzle across my ankle and resumed snoring.

I was more tired than I'd ever been in my life, but I couldn't sleep. I was too anxious. I sat in the dark thinking about everything that had happened and wondering what tomorrow would bring. Would there be a joyous reunion with Mom and Dad? Or would BeeBee and I learn that we were orphans? I loved Grandma and Grandpa, but I wanted Mom and Dad back.

The night dragged on. No more waves came.

Eventually I must have dozed off because when I opened my eyes, I saw the first hint of daylight. BeeBee had shifted away from me and lay on her side, curled around Pansy. Pansy's ears pricked up when I stirred. Her tail thumped the sand.

I moved my head from side to side, working the stiffness out of my neck. Then I looked at my burned right palm. It was blistered and red, but it didn't hurt as much as it had the night before.

The sun rose, bringing light and warmth and hope.

As soon as I stood up, BeeBee awoke. "Is it safe to go back?" she asked. "Did you hear the all-clear signal?"

"I didn't hear a signal, but I'm sure the tsunami is over."

"Good. I'm starving."

We walked through the sand, stepping over downed trees and going around an astonishing amount of debris. What had been a woods last night now looked more like a movie set for a film about the end of the world.

A woman's straw hat lay upside down, pink ribbons trailing across the sand. A portable barbecue was wedged into the ground. An inflatable raft with a crab pot still attached to a cord nested six feet up in a tree.

Pansy ran a short way ahead, then returned. It was clear that she wanted to stay close to us.

"Is that a refrigerator?" BeeBee asked.

I looked where she was pointing. A full-size white refrigerator had been plucked from a seaside cottage or a home in Fisher and deposited on top of the hill.

"Maybe there's something in it that we can eat," I said.

"Like cold Snickers bars."

We hurried to the refrigerator and opened the door. It was no colder inside the appliance than it was outside, but the shelves contained a package of sliced ham, a carton of eggs, a half loaf of bread, a quart of milk, and a jar of dill pickles.

Curious, I opened the egg carton. Not a single egg was broken.

"No Snickers," BeeBee said, "but we can make ham sandwiches."

"We can't eat the ham," I said. "The fridge has been off too long; we might get food poisoning. We can't drink the milk either, but we can eat the bread and the pickles."

We each wrapped a slice of bread around a dill pickle. I gave Pansy a piece of bread too, which she gobbled without chewing. I gave her a second piece.

"This bread is stale," BeeBee said. Then she smiled. "Maybe we should complain and ask for our money back."

"It could be worse," I said. "The fridge might have been full of cauliflower and spinach."

"I'm thirsty," BeeBee said. "Too bad whoever owns this refrigerator didn't keep bottled water or soft drinks on hand."

Unsure when we'd get a chance to eat again, I took the rest of the bread with us.

"Do you want me to carry the jar of pickles?" BeeBee asked.

"No. They're too salty. They'll make us even thirstier."

Pansy walked as if she were glued to my pant leg, whining and poking her nose at the bread bag, until I let her eat a third slice. BeeBee and I each ate another piece too. Stale bread was better than hunger pangs.

"Are you sure we're going the right way?" BeeBee asked. "This doesn't look anything like it did last night."

I looked in every direction. The sun was higher now, and the sunlight still came from behind us. That meant we were walking westward, toward the ocean. "This is right," I said. "We need to keep the sun at our backs."

A short while after we found the refrigerator, I spotted something green half-buried in the sand. Kicking at it with my foot, I uncovered a six-pack of 7-Up.

"How about a warm 7-Up for breakfast?" I asked.

"Yum, yum," said BeeBee. "Stale bread and warm 7-Up."

I still had the hotel towel, so I used it to wipe the sand off the tops of two cans. We each popped one open. The 7-Up fizzed over the top and ran down the side. It wasn't cold, but it tasted fantastic.

I wondered if it was okay for a dog to drink soda

pop. Since Pansy must be every bit as thirsty as we were, I decided to let her have some.

I cupped my left hand and poured some of my pop into it. Then I held my hand in front of Pansy, who lapped up some 7-Up, stopped in surprise, stuck her tongue in and out a couple of times, and then drank the rest, licking my hand to be sure she got it all.

Refreshed by the food and drink, we continued walking. Maybe Norm and Josie did survive, I thought. Daren too. It's easier to be optimistic when you're not hungry.

When we came to a clump of tall trees, Pansy stood at the base of the trees and yipped, a high excited bark. She ran behind the trees and came back with a piece of white fabric in her mouth, which she dropped at BeeBee's feet.

"She found Josie's handkerchief!" BeeBee said. "Josie let me use it last night, and I noticed the roses on it."

Pansy stood on her hind legs, put her front paws on the trunk of the largest tree, and yipped again.

BeeBee and I looked up into the branches. I half expected Norm and Josie to be perched on one of the limbs like two big birds, though I knew that was silly. Even if they had climbed a tree to escape the tsunami, they'd have come down by now.

"Norm and Josie must have been here," BeeBee said.

"Maybe they stood behind these trees, the way we stood behind that big cedar. Maybe the trees protected them."

"I bet that's what happened," BeeBee said. She put the handkerchief in her pants pocket. "I'll give this to Josie when I see her."

I hope you will, I thought. *Oh, I hope you will.*

We hurried on, expecting to come out of the last of the trees and see the wide area of low shrubs that had stretched from the park bench to the beginning of the woods. The woods ended, but now, instead of the open area, there was a sharp drop-off. The wave had washed away the whole west side of the hill.

"The road is gone," BeeBee said. "So is the bench."

We walked to within ten feet of the edge. "Don't go any closer," I said. "It might crumble."

As we looked at the destruction, Pansy ran off to one side, sniffing the sand. "What has Pansy found?" I asked, and went to find out.

"It's footprints!" I called. "Someone else has been here this morning!"

We squatted beside the footprints and saw that they were two different sizes. "Two people," BeeBee said.

I watched Pansy closely. If Norm and Josie had made those footprints, I thought Pansy would get all excited. She didn't. She smelled the footprints while we looked at them, but when we walked on, she came with us.

We could see the remains of the two hotels now, and we saw the beach, although the wooden steps that had led from the hotels to the beach were no longer there.

Gentle waves lapped the shore just as they had before the tsunami. It was as if the ocean had forgotten all about yesterday's violence and returned to business as usual.

"I see people!" BeeBee said.

Sure enough. People were walking on the beach.

"They're probably looking for souvenirs of the tsunami," she said.

"Or they're looking for survivors. Maybe Mom and Dad are down there!"

That possibility gave both of us a spurt of energy, and we looked for a way to get off the hill. With the road washed away, it took us awhile. Most of the way, we simply sat down and slid in the sand, letting Pansy get down as best she could. When we reached the bottom, we headed toward the remains of the Totem Pole Inn.

Anticipation and dread wrestled within me. Would we see Mom and Dad soon—or would we learn that the *Elegant Empress* had disappeared? I didn't know whether to rush forward or hang back.

BeeBee made the decision for me by taking off at a trot, with Pansy loping beside her. I had to run to catch up to them.

Two women saw us approaching and hurried toward us. "Were you up on the hill all night?" one of them asked. When I said yes, she held out a snapshot of a young man and said, "I'm looking for my nephew. Did you see him?"

"No. There was an older couple up there for awhile but we got separated from them. We never saw your nephew. I'm sorry."

"He worked at the Frontier Lodge," the woman said, "in the kitchen."

I wondered if he had made our pizza and the two milkshakes.

"Do you know anything about the *Elegant Empress*?" I asked.

"Who?"

"It's a ship. Our parents were on it when the

earthquake hit, and we don't know what happened to them."

"I haven't heard anything about a ship," the woman said.

"Nor have I," said her companion.

"Good luck," the woman said.

"I hope you find your nephew," BeeBee said.

We had similar conversations with other people. One was hunting for his son, who was a bellhop at the Totem Pole Inn. Another said her teenage daughter had been at a birthday party on the beach the night before. The third asked if we had seen any of the firefighters.

We disappointed each person with our answers—and they disappointed us with theirs.

"The power is still out in most of the county," the last man told us. "Phone lines are out too, and the cell phone tower washed away. I haven't heard a news broadcast since I came out here about two this morning, when a Portland station broadcast an all-clear."

We asked everyone we saw, but nobody knew what had happened to the *Elegant Empress*.

12

BeeBee and I walked slowly around the remains of the Totem Pole Inn. "If Mom and Dad are okay," I said, "I know they'll come here."

BeeBee poked at the ashes with a stick. "Bill's gone," she said.

Helicopters droned overhead, following the coastline.

A woman wearing an armband approached. "Do you need help?" she asked. "I'm with the emergency management service, and we're here to help survivors."

"We're looking for our parents."

"We're also looking for Pansy's owners," BeeBee said.

I told the woman what had happened to us.

"We have a temporary headquarters set up in a tent, only half a mile up the beach," she said. "Go there, and they'll give you something to eat and help you search the information we have, to see if your parents and your friends have been found."

"Thanks," I said.

We headed toward the tent.

"What if Mom and Dad haven't been found?" BeeBee asked.

"Then we'll keep looking for them. The emergency people probably have a computer network where names can be entered. We'll put our names in, so if Mom and Dad are searching for us somewhere else, they'll know we're okay." I sounded confident, but it was all an act.

"There's still no power," BeeBee said. "They could use laptops running on batteries to collect data, but without telephone lines they can't send that information elsewhere. How would the modem work?"

"Did Norm and Josie ever say their last name?" I asked.

"I don't think so. If they did, I don't remember it."

A long line of people stretched out of the tent. "Before we get in line," I said, "let's walk past everyone who's waiting, in case Mom and Dad are here."

We walked beside the line of people. My eyes

skimmed each face as I hoped desperately that the next one would be familiar.

None were.

When we reached the point where the line of people went inside the tent, there was a table where workers were serving sandwiches and juice.

"I'll look for Mom and Dad inside," BeeBee said. "You get us some food."

I took three sandwiches and two cans of juice. Soon BeeBee came back. "There are twelve people waiting inside," she reported, "plus the twenty-five in line outside, but I don't know any of them."

We took our place at the end of the line and started to eat. BeeBee was so glad to get decent food that she didn't even bother to pick the lettuce out of her sandwich.

I broke the third sandwich into pieces and gave them to Pansy.

"This is a *real* dog sandwich," BeeBee said, "Not like the one we made during the tsunami last night."

Last night. Less than half a day. I could hardly believe that so little time had passed since BeeBee and I had held Pansy between us while we hid behind the cedar tree. The night had seemed endless.

Yesterday morning at about this time, I had been

walking on the beach with Mom and Dad. We had read the warning sign and I had made my sea picture. It seemed like ten years ago, like a happy memory from when I was only three or four years old.

A fist jabbed me right between the shoulder blades. "Well, well," said a familiar voice. "The scaredy-cat made it through the big bad wave."

Last night I had hoped Daren would survive. Now that he was here, I had mixed feelings.

"I'm glad I went uphill," I said. "It saved my life."

"You were scared stiff," Daren said. "While you were running away, I walked down to the beach and waded in the water."

"What happened when the big waves came?" BeeBee asked.

"The first one picked me up and dropped me on top of the Totem Pole Inn's elevator tower. I clung to the edge of the roof when the wave receded."

"We saw the two people on the tower roof," I said, "but we couldn't tell who they were."

"It was me and a cook from the hotel. We found a trap door in the roof that went inside the tower to the elevator equipment. We stayed in there all night and climbed down this morning. We heard the second wave, but the concrete tower held."

"You were lucky," I said.

"Not lucky, just brave. I wasn't scared for one second."

Liar, I thought. *We were all scared.*

"You're the one who was afraid," Daren went on.

"Anyone with sense would be afraid of a tsunami," I said.

"Are you saying I don't have any sense?"

"I'm saying you were just as frightened as I was."

Daren raised his hand as if to punch me.

I pushed his hand away and looked him in the eye. "You were plenty scared yesterday," I said, "when you thought you were going to be burned alive in the hotel."

"I was never scared!"

"Then why were you yelling for help? Why did you rush past us in the stairway and push my sister down after we saved your life? You'd have been burned alive if I hadn't dragged you down the stairs with us."

"I didn't yell for help, and you didn't save me. What a joke! If you tell anyone that you saved my life, I'll swear you're making it up."

"He did too save you," BeeBee said, "and he has a witness. Don't forget: I was there."

"Why you little brat," Daren said. "I ought to . . ."

I took a step toward Daren, keeping BeeBee behind me. "Lay a hand on her, and you'll wish you hadn't," I said.

Daren's mouth actually dropped open. He looked the way cartoon characters look when they're surprised.

"That goes for next year at school too," I added. "Keep away from her."

"Are you threatening me?"

"That's right. I may be shorter than you are, but I'm smart, and if you don't quit bothering us, the whole state of Kansas is going to hear how you pushed an eight-year-old down in order to save yourself."

Daren gaped at me for a few seconds. Then he shrugged. "Hey, man," he said. "No need to get all worked into a twist."

I felt ten feet tall. Daren was backing down!

"You're alive because of me," I said. "You should be grateful."

He glared at me, but he didn't deny what I said. I knew we'd never be friends, and I knew my problems with Daren probably weren't over permanently, but I had taken a giant step on the road to solving them. Maybe I'd make my summer goals after all.

"Have you heard from your parents?" I asked. "Do you know what happened to the *Elegant Empress*?"

"No. I was on my way to the tent to ask about the ship when I saw you."

"This is the line for information," I said. "You can wait with us."

BeeBee gave me a surprised look. I was surprised too. I never thought I'd invite Daren to spend two seconds with me, but now that I had finally confronted him, he had lost his power over me. He was just another kid looking for his parents, the same as we were.

"Where did you get the sandwich?" Daren asked.

I told him, and he left to get some food.

"Thanks for sticking up for me," BeeBee said.

"If he ever bothers you again, tell me." I smiled, remembering the conversation.

"I wonder why he acted ashamed of being scared when the hotel was on fire," BeeBee said. "I was scared."

"So was I. Who wouldn't be?"

We had waited in the line half an hour when Pansy gave an excited "Yip!" and took off down the beach. She ran in circles around the man walking toward us, leaping in the air with joy.

"It's Norm!" BeeBee said.

"Norm!" I called, waving my hands over my head.

BeeBee ran to him and threw her arms around him. Together they returned to where I waited in line.

"I'm so glad to see you," Norm said, wiping tears from his wrinkled cheeks. "And Pansy!" He picked the wriggling dog up and hugged her. "We let her go last night, figuring she'd follow you kids. We wanted her to be safe even if we didn't make it."

"Where's Josie?" BeeBee asked.

"She's gone," Norm said, his voice breaking. "When we heard that second big wave coming, I climbed up a tree and pulled Josie up after me. When the wave hit us, I was able to hang on but Josie couldn't. The force of the water was too much for her. She lost her grip and was swept away."

Norm stroked the dog, unable to talk for a moment. "I thought of going with her," he said. "We were together forty-seven years, and it would have been easy to release my hold on the tree and let the water take me too. But then I thought about our son and our grandkids. I'd like to see those grandkids grow up. I worried about Pansy too. She needs me to look after her."

"I'm sorry about Josie," I said. "I liked her a lot."

"I *loved* her," BeeBee said. "I have her handkerchief. Pansy found it this morning." BeeBee held the handkerchief toward Norm.

"You keep that, honey," Norm said. "Think of my Josie whenever you use it."

"Thank you." BeeBee folded the handkerchief carefully and tucked it in her pocket.

"You kids saved Pansy's life," Norm said.

"And she saved ours," I replied. "She barked to let us know when the second wave was coming, and we hid behind a big tree."

Norm stood with us while we waited in line. He told us that his house had been destroyed by the tsunami. "One of the firefighters helped me get down the hill," he said. "He managed to stay afloat on a beam from the hotel during the first wave, then swam ashore and ran up the hill before the second wave hit. He found me as soon as it got light, and we came down together."

"We saw footprints," BeeBee said. "We knew someone else had been in the woods."

The line moved slowly. We had not yet reached the entrance to the tent when a man with a megaphone came out and shouted an announcement: "If any of you are here to inquire about passengers on the *Elegant Empress*, please follow me."

BeeBee, Daren, and I hurried toward the man. So did several other people who had been waiting in the line. When we were all grouped around the man with the megaphone, he said, "I have good news for you. The *Elegant Empress* was far enough away from shore that it was able to ride the tsunami waves without capsizing. All passengers and crew are safe."

"Wasn't the ship damaged?" someone asked.

"No. The captain waited until the all-clear signal was radioed to him and then . . ."

The man kept talking, but I found it hard to concentrate on his words. They were safe! Mom and Dad were alive!

When I tuned in again, I heard him say, "The captain kept the *Elegant Empress* out until daybreak because he knew the Fisher Beach dock where he normally arrives and departs was destroyed, and he didn't want to dock someplace new in the dark. He traveled twenty miles north before he found a suitable dock that was intact. He's now landed safely, and the passengers are getting off."

"If the phone lines are still out, how do you know all that?" BeeBee asked.

"Emergency workers have mobile radios that run on vehicle batteries, plus we have a network of ham radio operators. A TV news crew has a satellite link, and we're getting reports from their helicopter too."

When we looked for Norm to tell him our good news, we found him with a younger man.

"This is my son, Arnie," Norm said. "He's invited me and Pansy to stay with him and his family for a while."

"Thank you again for helping us last night," I said. "Here's your flashlight."

"We'll always remember you and Josie," BeeBee said.

Even though we had known the elderly couple for only a few hours, I knew BeeBee was right. We would never forget their kindness.

An hour later, Mom and Dad arrived in a yellow school bus that had been pressed into service. Daren's parents were with them. Mom cried when she saw us, and I admit I had a lump in my throat too.

The governor declared the whole Oregon coast a disaster area. Since we had lost all of our clothes and luggage, as well as our hotel room, we decided to fly home as soon as we could. By seven o'clock that night, we had ridden to Portland and booked a flight back to Kansas.

Alexander the Greatest was glad we came home early. He rubbed around my ankles, purring his pleasure. As I poured fresh water in his bowl, Mom said, "Dad and I are proud of how you acted in an emergency, Kyle. We've decided to raise your allowance."

All right! I did a victory dance around the kitchen.

"What about my allowance?" BeeBee asked. "I was brave too."

"You were brave," Mom agreed, "but Kyle's the one who made the decisions. He was responsible."

To my surprise, BeeBee didn't argue.

With my increased wealth, I bought BeeBee a new teddy bear. I thought she'd name it Bill Junior, but she didn't. She named it Dollar Bill.

A couple of weeks later, I started seventh grade. I never did get my batting average where I wanted it, but I ended the season batting .235, which was fifteen points higher than the year before, and I made two double plays as a shortstop. I didn't learn to pop a wheelie on my scooter either, although I skinned up my arms and legs trying.

On the first day of school, my new language arts teacher assigned a report. We were each supposed to write about our summer vacation.

During lunch recess, Gary and I were kicking a soccer ball around when Daren walked toward us.

"Here comes trouble," Gary muttered as he picked up the ball. "Let's get out of here."

"It's okay," I said. "He won't bother us."

Gary looked skeptical, but I stayed where I was.

Daren stopped beside me. "Are you going to do your report on the trip to Oregon?" he asked.

"Yes."

"If we tell everything that happened that night," Daren said, "nobody will believe us."

"Especially the part about you landing on the elevator tower during a tsunami. That was amazing."

"Amazing," he said, "but true."

And then the really amazing thing happened: Daren Hazelton actually smiled at me. I thought Gary was going to faint.

"I'm going to call my report, 'The Terrible Trip,'" Daren said.

"It was the worst vacation ever," I agreed, but I knew the trip hadn't been all bad. I wasn't afraid of Daren anymore.

Author's Note

Thousands of people have been killed by Pacific Ocean tsunamis, and scientists fear that more giant waves will hit in the future.

The west coast of the United States is vulnerable to tsunamis because there is a nine hundred mile-long crack in the earth's crust offshore. This crack can create powerful earthquakes which displace the sea floor and result in waves that travel up to six hundred miles per hour and rise to one hundred feet in height.

Tsunamis can occur at any time of the day or night, in any kind of weather condition. The first waves may reach shore within minutes after the earthquake—or they may not hit for several hours.

My research for this book included two trips to Pacific coast towns, one in Oregon and one in Washington, where I gathered tsunami information and followed the evacuation signs.

In Washington the state Emergency Management

Division posts "Tsunami Hazard Zone" signs instructing people what to do in case of an earthquake. Tsunami evacuation routes are clearly marked to show coastal residents and visitors the best way to get inland, and to higher ground. Community programs seek to educate people about how to protect themselves in the event of a tsunami.

In Oregon no schools or hospitals can be built near the shore, and evacuation drills are held in many areas. Beaches have signs telling how to escape a tsunami.

There has been controversy over the best way to alert people when an official tsunami warning is issued. Some towns prefer not to use sirens because the meaning is often misinterpreted, especially by visitors. The idea of using cows came from the town of Cannon Beach, Oregon, which uses mooing instead of a siren as a tsunami warning.

The National Oceanic and Atmospheric Administration (NOAA) Weather Radio broadcasts emergency tsunami information as well as shelter locations.

Other helpful sources of information were:

Killer Wave: Power of the Tsunami, a video produced by National Geographic in 1997

Author's Note

Tsunami: The Underrated Hazard by Edward Bryant
(Cambridge University Press, 2001)
Tsunami! by Walter Dudley and Min Lee
(University of Hawaii Press, 1988)
Publications from the Washington State Emergency
Management Division
National Oceanic and Atmospheric Administration,
www.noaa.gov
"Tsunami: The Great Waves"
www.nws.noaa.gov/om/brochures/tsunami.htm

About the Author

Peg Kehret's books for young readers are regularly recommended by the American Library Association, the International Reading Association, and the Children's Book Council. She has won twenty-one state children's choice awards and has also won the Golden Kite Award from the Society of Children's Book Writers & Illustrators and the PEN Center West Award for Children's Literature. A longtime volunteer at the Humane Society, she often uses animals in her stories. Peg won the Henry Bergh Award from the American Society for the Prevention of Cruelty to Animals for *Saving Lilly*.

Peg and her husband, Carl, live in a log house on ten acres of forest near Mount Rainier National Park. Their property is a sanctuary for black-tailed deer, elk, rabbits, and many kinds of birds. They have two grown children, four grandchildren, a dog, and two cats. When she is not writing, Peg likes to read, watch baseball, and pump her old player piano.